"You're quite safe."

Roderick continued. "I got the message last night. 'Admire me, but don't expect anything more.' Right?"

Flower blushed hotly. "That isn't fair. I did nothing to encourage you."

"You'd been sending out encouraging signals all evening, my dear."

At the point of denying it, she realized that perhaps it was true. Then, recovering her self-possession, she said coldly, "I won't deny that I found you attractive—at first. But since I've gotten to know you, I've revised my opinion."

Instead of being crushed by her put-down, he grinned. "I haven't revised mine of you. I still think you're ravishing, and I suppose, if you insist, we'll postpone the inevitable for a few days."

"It is not inevitable! I have no intention of going to bed with you—*ever*."

Anne Weale and her husband live in a Spanish villa high above the Mediterranean. An active woman, Anne enjoys swimming, interior decorating and antique hunting. But most of all, she loves traveling. Researching new romantic backgrounds, she has explored New England, Florida, Canada, Australia, Italy, the Caribbean and the Pacific.

Books by Anne Weale

ANTIGUA KISS
FLORA
SUMMER'S AWAKENING

HARLEQUIN ROMANCE

HARLEQUIN PRESENTS

THE SINGING TREE
Anne Weale

Harlequin Books

TORONTO • NEW YORK • LONDON
AMSTERDAM • PARIS • SYDNEY • HAMBURG
STOCKHOLM • ATHENS • TOKYO • MILAN
MADRID • WARSAW • BUDAPEST • AUCKLAND

Reference in this book is made to
MARRIAGE IS A LOVING BUSINESS
by Paul A. Hauck,
published in the United States
by Westminster/John Knox Press.

Original hardcover edition published in 1992
by Mills & Boon Limited

ISBN 0-373-03257-9

Harlequin Romance first edition March 1993

THE SINGING TREE

CHAPTER ONE

DEPENDING on the state of the traffic, it took about an hour for Flower to drive from the flat in London her grandfather had given her for her twenty-first birthday to the rambling country mansion which, for the past twelve years, he had leased from an aristocratic family too hard up to continue to live there themselves.

Flower had been ten when the old man had moved into Bosanquet Manor with his son and his daughter-in-law and their two children, soon to be orphaned by a tragic accident.

Now she was nearly twenty-three, the much-indulged grandchild of one of the richest men in England. Spoilt, some people would have called her. She had everything money could buy.

Her car was a scarlet Ferrari, the three-litre Mondial coupé, one of the most sophisticated pieces of engineering available to the privileged few who could afford it. Her watch was a handmade gold Reverso by Jaeger-Le-Coultre with her monogram 'F J D' engraved on the pivoting case. She bought her clothes in Milan, Paris and the most expensive shops in London.

What very few people knew was that, when she was in her late teens, Flower had suffered two serious reverses. At that age such things were deeply wounding. Although superficially healed, those early hurts had left scars.

Towards the end of her schooling she had set her sights on becoming a designer, an ambition encouraged by the school's careers adviser. But her grandfather had insisted that, after a year at finishing-school in Switzerland, she should lead the frivolous party-going life of the débutantes of the 1930s.

For a long time she hadn't understood why, when he often spoke with contempt of the way the idle rich had ignored the plight of the poor when he was a teenager before World War II, he had forced her to become a social butterfly.

Only later had she come to understand that it gave him a deep satisfaction to have a granddaughter who didn't work for her living.

At the time she had protested, argued, cajoled, pleaded, even threatened to run away. Whereupon the old man had warned her that, if she did, he would not only cut off her allowance but also forbid her brother Stephen, who worked for him, to help her or even to see her.

In the end she had capitulated. At sixteen she had not been strong enough to defy someone she loved. For the strange thing was that, in spite of the unfair means he had used to bend her to his will, he had not destroyed her love for him. Although many people disliked Abel Dursley, and she could understand why, Flower herself had loved her grandfather from babyhood and always would.

But the frustration and misery he had inflicted on her when she was sixteen had been nothing compared with the anguish, only two years later, of her first real-life love-affair.

Before that, the man of her dreams had not been a living person. She had never spent time daydreaming about pop stars, actors or athletes. Her heart-throb had been Piers Anstruther who had been born at the manor in 1613 and died fighting for King Charles I at the Battle of Naseby in 1645.

Flower had never told anyone—not even Emily Fairchild, her only close friend—about her teenage fantasies about the blue-eyed Cavalier whose portrait hung in the dining-room. Or that they had never quite lost their hold on her imagination.

She knew it was ridiculous still to compare every man she met with the devil-may-care Royalist whose features gazed down at her every night at dinner.

He had been the younger, unmarried son of the titled landowner whose descendants had continued to live at Bosanquet until two generations of misfortune had forced the present owner to vacate the family home and take his invalid wife to a warmer, drier climate.

Surely, somewhere in the world, there must be a living man whose chin was as strong, whose mouth as firmly cut, whose eyes were as merry and amorous as those of Colonel Piers Anstruther?

But if there was such a man she had yet to catch a glimpse of him, let alone meet him.

Which was not to say that she had never been attracted to anyone. She had. For several years, after her first disillusionment, her relationships with the opposite sex had provided fodder for the gossip columnists. But always, always there had been something she couldn't take about the men with whom her name had been linked. One had lacked any sense of humour. Another had been a snob who had made the mistake of patronising her grandfather.

There were times when Flower herself wished that Abel Dursley would eat less noisily and belch more discreetly at the end of a meal. But if anyone else showed disdain for his rough-diamond ways her grey eyes would sparkle with anger. She not only loved the old man; she admired his achievements and the immense strength of will which had lifted him from rags to riches.

As she drove home one autumn afternoon, after two days of concentrated shopping, she was thinking about her friend Emily, now pregnant for the second time since her youthful marriage to Andrew, her childhood sweetheart.

Emily could never believe that Flower envied her. Without wishing for such a life herself, her friend thought it must be marvellous for Flower to have the flat and the lavish allowance, and every winter to spend a month skiing and another month in the sunny West Indies.

What Emily didn't realise, thought Flower as the Ferrari zoomed along the motorway, was that a picnic on a park bench with the right man was more exciting than dining on lobster and champagne and dancing under a Caribbean moon with the wrong one.

Even the pleasure of wearing the new clothes in the pile of boxes beside her would be diminished by the fact that there was no man she wanted to attract. At the moment her love-life was a void; and, with her twenty-third birthday coming up in a few months' time, she was beginning to feel she was destined to be single forever.

This would not have mattered had she had a career to occupy her. But with nothing to do except enjoy herself, and no one but Emily—now living in the north of England—with whom to share her deepest feelings, she often felt lonely and without any purpose in life.

It was late afternoon and the light was beginning to fade when, from a couple of miles away, she glimpsed the ancient stone walls and tall twisted chimneys of the manor.

Originally it had been a convent, and the building still contained the refectory where the nuns had eaten their meals and the calefactory or warming-room where, in the bitter winters of the thirteenth and fourteenth centuries, they had sometimes been allowed to sit by the fire.

Like all the religious houses in England, the convent had been closed down by the six-times-married King Henry the Eighth and subsequently sold for eight hundred pounds to Piers Anstruther's grandfather. In the following centuries his descendants had made many alterations to the property, adding wings and towers and fine oriel windows until now it was one of the most beautiful manor houses in the whole of England.

Flower loved the place. Each time she came back from London the sight of it reminded her of a line from a poem learned at school—'a haunt of ancient peace'.

When the sleek scarlet car drew up in front of the house that had been home for more than half her lifetime, another vehicle was parked on the gravelled sweep, an undistinguished saloon bearing the insignia of a well-known car-rental firm.

Flower wondered who was visiting her grand-father in a hired car. Overseas guests were in-variably met at the airport by the second Rolls-

Royce and, as far as she knew, Abel wasn't expecting visitors.

The electronic device which opened the main gates to members of the household—other people had to announce themselves on an intercom—had also signalled her arrival in the staff quarters.

As she opened the driver's door and swung out long booted legs, a young footman came out of the house.

'Good evening, miss.'

'Hello, John. How's your cold?'

'Better, thank you, miss.'

Flower gave him her keys. 'Whose is that?' she asked, with a nod at the other car.

'I couldn't say, miss. I've just this minute come on duty and, Mr Watson being on the telephone, I haven't spoken to him yet.'

Watson was the butler. None of the servants had been in service with the Anstruthers. They had all been engaged by her grandfather through an agency for staff in London.

Leaving John to deal with her luggage and shopping and, later, to drive the car round to the garage in the former stable block, she went inside the house.

Before leaving London she had been to her hairdresser, who had added some silvery streaks to her naturally ash-blonde long hair and styled it in a silky mane which was not à la mode this autumn, but which suited the shape of her face, with its broad intelligent forehead concealed by a feathery fringe and obstinate jawline redeemed by a full, tender mouth.

At eighteen, nineteen and twenty, she had subscribed to every passing vogue. But now, having found her style, she ignored the vagaries of fashion unless they happened to suit her.

With one brief glance in a mirror to check that her lipstick was in order, she made her way to the drawing-room, a large and beautiful apartment not improved by the addition of two enormous velvet chesterfields and a number of over-stuffed arm-chairs upholstered in royal blue—which was Abel's favourite colour—and whose bulbous shapes he preferred to the elegance of Hepplewhite and Chippendale.

The terms of his lease forbade him to make any structural alterations to the manor, but many of the Anstruthers' furnishings had been consigned to the attics during his tenure and replaced with expensive modern pieces totally out of keeping with the style of the rooms, but which he thought an improvement.

Flower, whose taste had been educated during her visits to Emily's house during the holidays from the boarding-school where they had met, had had difficulty in hiding her dismay when, during her absence, the charming four-poster in her room had been changed for a pop-starish round bed with a headboard incorporating various gadgets.

She had often wondered why her grandfather wanted to live in a historic house when he showed no appreciation of its finer points. He could have built an extravagant new house which would have served him much better in terms of comfort and convenience.

The explanation seemed to be that living at Bosanquet Manor gave him a sense of being not merely equal but superior to the class which, during his boyhood, had represented unattainable heights

of power and grandeur. Now he was the top dog
and they—as represented by the Anstruthers—were
the underdogs.

To Flower, born two generations later, the social
injustices of her grandfather's youth were a thing
of the past and better forgotten. She felt rather sorry
for the dispossessed Anstruthers.

When she entered the drawing-room she found
Abel ensconced in one of his royal-blue armchairs,
holding a large cigar and speaking to a man who
was seated with his back to the door.

Her grandfather did not rise from his chair when
he saw her but she was aware that the visitor did,
although she did not glance at him until she had
greeted the old man with a smiling, 'I'm back. How
are you, darling?' and a kiss on the top of his bald
head.

'Not too bad. Have you had a good time?'

'Mm . . . super.' She turned her smile on the man
who was with him, the driver of the hired car.

The smile vanished from her face. Her eyes
widened in disbelief.

Shorn of his dark flowing hair and curling
moustache, and divested of his lace collar, there
stood the hero of her girlish daydreams, Piers
Anstruther. Well over six feet tall, with shoulders
in proportion to his height, he was looking down
at her with eyes so astonishingly blue that she
realised the colours of the painting must have faded.
But instead of looking amused, as he had while his
portrait was painted, his expression now seemed
rather stern.

'This is. young Anstruther, Flower. He's come
over from the States,' said her grandfather.

He did not complete the introduction but left it to the younger man to say, 'How do you do, Miss Dursley?' and offer a lean suntanned hand.

Flower was still confused by his almost incredible likeness to the portrait. She felt he was Piers come to life, or Piers' ghost; and as she responded to his gesture she was half afraid that before their fingers touched he would evaporate.

But the hand which closed firmly over hers was unmistakably flesh and blood.

Pulling herself together, she said, 'You ... you must forgive me for staring at you. It's just that you're so incredibly like the picture in the dining-room ... your ancestor Piers Anstruther. What brings you to England, Mr Anstruther?'

'Mr Dursley's letter to my father, offering to buy the house when the lease ends in nine months' time,' was his somewhat curt answer. 'My father died a few weeks ago. The house is mine now. I don't wish to sell it—or to renew the lease.'

'As to that, I've an option to extend it for a further five years, which you'll find it expensive to contest in a court of law,' said Abel with rather malicious satisfaction.

Kind and generous when things went smoothly, he could be very unpleasant if his wishes were thwarted. Although nowadays not many people were in a position to thwart him.

As Flower sat down the other man resumed his seat. 'I hope that won't be necessary.'

If his father had died, he was no longer Mr Anstruther but Sir Whatever-his-name-was, she realised, looking him over.

He was dressed with comfortable casualness in a pale khaki cotton windcheater over a thin navy

jersey and a blue cotton shirt, probably bought or
mail ordered from Brooks Brothers' shop in New
York. Straight-legged trousers and soft leather
loafers, immaculately polished, completed a mode
of dress she recognised as what Americans called
the preppie look.

His thick dark hair was brushed back and
touched the collar of his shirt but was cut short in
front of his ears. He had the slight five o'clock
shadow of a gypsy-dark skin which took a tan
quickly and easily. She could not see his teeth at
the moment but she had no doubt they were those
of someone who had always had regular checks and
never eaten much sweet stuff.

She put his age somewhere near thirty, and she
seemed to have a vague memory that, at the time
his parents had gone to live abroad, he had still
been at Eton, the famous public school where generations of Anstruthers had been educated.
Somehow, in spite of their financial difficulties, his
parents had contrived to continue that family
tradition.

'Have you asked for tea, Dodo?' she asked her
grandfather.

'You said you wouldn't be late so I told Watson
we'd 'ave it as soon as you arrived. He ought to
have brought it by now. Give him a buzz, will you,
Flower?'

In her first term at boarding-school Flower's
name had added to her unhappiness. The other girls
had pretended to think it was spelt 'flour' and had
made unkind jokes about it and about Dursley pork
pies and her grandfather's other food products. She
had longed to be called Jane or Mary instead of

what one girl had called 'a silly, made-up, film star's name'.

It was Emily's mother who had told her this was not true; her 'lovely and unusual' name had been popular in the eighteenth century but used only rarely since then.

Before she could use the house telephone Abel had installed in every room the double doors opened and Watson entered with the tea-tray. He was followed by John, who closed the doors and quickly arranged a table beside her chair.

'What part of America have you come from?' she asked their visitor while these preparations were going on.

'From New York.'

She thought he was going to leave it at that but, after a brief pause, he went on, 'My parents lived in Arizona, where the very dry climate improved my mother's health for some years. Have you been to America, Miss Dursley?'

'Only to Palm Beach one winter. The shops were stunning but the average age was about eighty.'

'So I should imagine.'

He looked away, his blue gaze scanning the room he had last seen in his teens.

She could understand his interest in it. At the same time she felt slightly piqued by his clear lack of interest in her. She was not vain, but she was a striking young woman who made the most of her assets, and she was accustomed to receiving some tacit acknowledgment of the fact.

As far as this man was concerned she might have been Abel's sixty-year-old spinster sister rather than his granddaughter. He didn't seem to have noticed that she had a good figure, long legs and an unblemished creamy complexion which more than one man had told her he'd wanted to stroke from the moment they were introduced.

'Did your wife come over with you?' she asked, seeking a reason for his indifference.

'I'm not married.'

'In that case I don't see your objection to renewing my lease,' said her grandfather. 'If you were a family man I could understand it. But a bachelor's got no need for a place this size. Unless the fact of the matter is that you've found an American girl whose father is willing to pay to keep it up in return for her being a Lady?'

Fortunately Watson and John had left the room by this time. Even so, inwardly Flower winced at Abel's crudity. He shouldn't have said that. It would only put the younger man's back up.

To his credit however, whatever distaste he felt privately, the owner of the house did not show it. He said levelly, 'I am not engaged to be married, and my father thought it inappropriate to use his title in America. As far as the legal side of the situation is concerned, I believe it's possible that, as the property is entailed, your option might have been valid only while my father was alive, Mr Dursley.'

Flower saw her grandfather's neck begin to swell, his ruddy face become more purple.

She said hastily, 'I think we should have tea now. There'll be plenty of time to talk later. I assume you are spending the night here, Sir...I don't know your first name.'

'Roderick.'

'Which was your room when you lived here, Sir Roderick?' she enquired.

'The third one along the west corridor. It has a stuffed leopard in it.'

'I expect you'd like to sleep there tonight, although I'm afraid the leopard is now in the attics. It's not everyone's idea of a fun thing to have in a bedroom,' she said with a grin.

For the first time she saw a responsive gleam of amusement in the vivid dark-lashed blue eyes.

'No, I dare say you're right—although, when I was a schoolboy, I thought it the finest thing in the house. It was shot by one of my great-uncles in the days when killing wild animals was an acceptable activity.'

'The thing I like best of all is the black and gold chair with swan's-neck arms,' she told him. 'It's in my room. I don't sit on it. The caning is brittle with age. I just like to have it there and look at it.'

She was trying to establish a rapport. Her instinct told her that bullying—her grandfather's favourite weapon—would never work with Roderick Anstruther. He would have to be persuaded to change his mind or, at worst, to agree to a compromise.

'There's no need to put me up. I should like to look over the place, if I may, but I can stay at the pub,' he said.

'They aren't doing bed and breakfast any more, and we shouldn't dream of allowing you to stay anywhere but here. When did you arrive in England?' In her desire to keep the conversation going while her grandfather's hot temper cooled Flower's next question came without thinking. 'Did you come over on Concorde or by the longer flight?'

He said drily, 'I managed to get a stand-by ticket for the night flight...if you know what a stand-by is, Miss Dursley.'

For the first time since she had entered the room he gave her a brief but comprehensive scrutiny. As his cool eyes swept from her newly done hair to the toes of her Italian boots she knew intuitively that he had her pegged as a decorative but empty-headed rich girl, pampered from birth and with little idea how the other half lived.

Her own hackles rising a fraction, she said crisply, 'Of course. For anyone travelling alone, stand-bys are a marvellous saving. Did you have to wait long?'

'Not long.'

'Even so, the flight itself is tiring. I remember being terribly jet lagged when we came back from Palm Beach on a night flight.'

'You probably ate the meal and watched the movie. I slept all the way over.'

'All the comings and goings didn't disturb you? And the lack of space—especially for someone of your size?'

'Nothing disturbs a moonlighter when he gets a chance to get his head down. I could sleep on a crowded sidewalk.'

Although his years in America had not altered his English accent, they had obviously made him adopt American usage.

'What's a moonlighter?' she asked.

'Someone who supplements his income with a second job. Here, I believe, it's more often a means of evading tax than a financial necessity as it has been in my case.'

Abel said, 'If you're that hard-pressed for money I'm damned if I see how you think you can live here. I reckon you've no idea what it costs. The 'eating alone will set you back six thousand a year, never mind the bill for repairs. It's a constant expense, a place this size. You need my kind of income to live in a mansion these days. Otherwise you're sunk before you start.'

Sir Roderick listened in silence. While he had been conversing with Flower he had done what a good host should have done, although it would never have occurred to Abel to wait on anyone. He had taken her grandfather's cup and saucer and a plate to him, and offered the sandwiches to him before replacing them near Flower and helping himself to two or three.

Now he sat quietly, eating and drinking, while her grandfather tried to hector him; and, though his tanned face expressed nothing but civil attention to what was being said to him, she sensed that he was as implacable in his determination to repossess the house as her grandfather was to hang on to it.

'Perhaps you've got it in mind to open the place to the public?' Abel said presently. 'That's no simple solution, let me tell you. I've been into the matter. I know what I'm talking about. You need about fifty thousand visitors a year to break even, never mind make a profit. I doubt if you'd get half that number, not without a lot of expensive advertising and investing in various attractions. A house of this size by itself doesn't have enough drawing power.'

He leaned forward, wagging his finger. 'It's estates that keep these big houses in the black, and here there is no estate. Your great grandfather sold most of it off to meet his losses from gambling, so I'm told. And what little was left of the land was got rid of later by your granddad. A right pair of fools, by the sound of it.'

For the second time Flower caught a glimpse of a fleeting gleam of amusement in their visitor's summer-sky eyes.

'You don't mince your words, Mr Dursley.'

'No, I don't...never did,' agreed Abel. 'I'm a plain-speaking man of the people, and proud of it. I never had any advantages when I was young. In fact, I'm not ashamed to say that I came from what in them days was called a slum. Inner cities, they call them now, but it's the same thing. I knew nippers who went to school barefoot and I only had a pair of gym shoes...winter and summer...'

As he warmed to his theme, Flower clenched her teeth on a yawn. She had heard all this many times before, and no story bore constant retelling.

She began to think about what to wear for dinner. Not anything too elaborate, because for all she knew their guest might have brought nothing with him but a change of trousers and some clean shirts. All the same, his unexpected presence made her review her new clothes with an excitement which had been lacking earlier.

Presently, taking advantage of one of her grandfather's pauses for breath to offer him another cup of tea and anticipating, correctly, that their visitor would again wait on the old man, she said, 'If you'll give me your keys, Sir Roderick, I'll go and arrange for your luggage to be brought in and have your bedroom prepared for you.'

'Are you sure it's not inconvenient?'

'Not in the least.'

He handed over an ignition key with the tag of the car-hire company.

'And the keys to your luggage?'

'I have only hand-luggage with me. My grip isn't locked.'

About an hour later, after their visitor had gone up to his room to have a shower before dinner, Abel said, 'You know what he really wants, don't you? Cheeky young whipper-snapper! Not to live 'ere. Not on your nelly! What he wants is to screw some more cash out of me.'

'You may be right about that, but he certainly isn't a whipper-snapper, Dodo. He's six-feet-two if he's an inch. Anyway, considering the rate of inflation since the original lease was signed, surely he's entitled to more money? Everything else has gone up. Why not our rent?

'Because I'm already paying a king's ransom to keep the place insured and repaired. It was close to the works, and convenient, but I reckon now I'd have done better to find a place I could buy. If it hadn't been for the entail his father would have sold it to me.'

The works he referred to were an enormous flour-mill surrounded by a complex of bakeries making every kind of bread and pastry. It was the heart of his empire, and from it a fleet of vehicles, decorated with scenes of harvest fields, country kitchens and happy, healthy families, delivered his wares to supermarkets and shops all over England.

His brand was a household name blazoned on roadside hoardings and on the advertisement panels in the London Underground, and brought into millions of homes by commercial television.

'I haven't made many mistakes in my life, but I reckon that was one of them,' he went on in a sombre tone. 'I'm too old now to want to move again.'

'Do you think he may be right about the option to renew being invalidated by his father's death?'

'I don't know, I'll have it looked into first thing tomorrow.'

He struggled to his feet from the deep armchair. Always a hearty trencherman, he was many pounds overweight and had been advised to reduce and to cut down on cigars and brandy. However, he chose to ignore his doctor's advice and tonight it struck Flower that he looked somewhat under the weather.

'Are you all right, Dodo?' she asked concernedly. 'You look awfully tired this evening.'

'Had a poor night last night. There's no need to fuss over me.'

His tone was brusque, making her suspect that he didn't feel well but wouldn't admit it.

'I'd sleep better if I had more confidence in your brother's abilities,' he added with a frown. 'He's not putting his back into the job. I can't rely on his judgement.'

This, too, was a recurring theme. Stephen Dursley, three years Flower's senior, was the old man's natural successor as chairman of the company. But Stephen was being forced to play a role for which he had no real aptitude.

She was glad to escape to her bedroom and relax in a warm bubble-bath, with her hair piled inside a large lacy bath-cap.

There were other things she wanted to think about rather than the battles between her brother and grandfather. She wondered how long Roderick

Anstruther was planning to spend in England and
if, though neither married nor engaged to be
married, he had an unofficial partner.

She didn't know much about his mind yet, but
physically he was undeniably attractive. Tall, well-
built, with long-fingered hands which looked
capable of crushing strength but which had handled
the fragile porcelain tea-service with none of her
grandfather's clumsiness.

Both Abel and Stephen were noisy men; bangers
of doors, rattlers of teaspoons, shouters. She supposed she took after her mother who, according to
Abel—who had never thought much of his
daughter-in-law—had been 'a bundle of nerves'. At
any rate, Flower preferred quietness to clamour.
The loud, aggressive way her brother drove his
Porsche was always an irritation to her, and his
liking, before his marriage, for the noisiest discos
was something she had never shared.

Revivals of schmaltzy numbers from the twenties
and thirties appealed to her more than current hits.
She adored 'Begin the Beguine,' sung by Julio
Iglesias, the good-looking Spanish pop star who was
also a qualified lawyer. This afternoon in the car
she had heard another song she liked.

She began to hum it, her quick ear for a tune
making it easier to remember the melody than the
lyric. But she could remember one line. 'When we
met, I felt my life begin...

And that, she realised with a start, was precisely
what she was feeling at this moment. That just now,
downstairs in the drawing-room, her life had entered a new phase.

At last, when she had more or less given up hope
of meeting anyone like him, the idol of her teenage

fantasies had materialised; not merely a passable likeness to the man of her dreams, but a replica of him.

How extraordinary that, after an interval of three hundred years, the genes which had shaped Piers Anstruther should be duplicated in his descendant. Or, perhaps, not as strange as it seemed. It could be that the vivid blue eyes and the hard lines of cheekbone and jaw had occurred in other Anstruthers whose faces had not been recorded by portrait-painter or miniaturist.

'When we met, I felt my life begin...' As she sang the snatch of the song she knew that she wasn't in love yet. But she could be...tomorrow or next week...if Roderick Anstruther's nature was as attractive as his looks.

She was ready for love, ripe for it. Now that she had given up hankering after a career as a designer her only other ambition in life was to be married. With two or three adorable tots whose childhood she would make much happier than her own had been.

Roy and Josie Dursley, her parents, had not been a well-matched couple. She could remember hearing their raised, angry voices in the sitting-room below her bedroom when they had lived in the suburbs.

Before the accident in which they had lost their lives she had been at a day school. Afterwards her grandfather had transferred her to a boarding-school. For one term she had been miserably homesick. But the next term Emily had arrived and a friendship had blossomed which they still kept up with frequent letters.

Emily had been in love with Andrew since she was thirteen years old, but he had not taken her seriously until she was eighteen. Now, when Flower went to stay with them, it made her ache with longing to experience the happiness they shared.

Perhaps today, at long last, she was on the threshold of it.

Steady on: you don't know this man yet. He may be a prize rat, she warned herself as she rose from the winking froth of bubbles, her slim body still slightly golden from a week at Cap Ferrat on the French Riviera at the beginning of September.

No longer as agonisingly potent as it had once been, the five-year-old memory of her first abortive love-affair sent a pang of remembered humiliation through her.

The man had been a fortune-hunter, attracted by her grandfather's millions, not by the naïve girl who had fallen headlong in love with him.

Although, looking back, she knew that her feeling for him had never been the deep lasting love she had thought it was at the time.

Like many girls of that age, she had been more in love with love than with the man concerned. And afterwards, afraid of being hurt again, she had carefully avoided any serious entanglements.

Until now...

CHAPTER TWO

No GIRL in her right mind, thought Flower as she puffed Rive Gauche into the air and twirled through the sensual vapour to envelop her hair and her person in an aura of delicious French fragrance, no girl with a particle of sense would not dress to the top of her bent when a man who might be *the* man had suddenly walked into her life.

But, instead of wearing any of the new things she had bought in London, she went down to dinner in a pair of black velvet Italian knee-breeches several seasons old, and a shirt of hand-embroidered white voile with ruffles at the neck and wrists.

The breeches were no longer high fashion but, worn with the sheerest of black tights and low-heeled black velvet slippers, they were still extremely becoming to her long slender legs and neat hips.

Her grandfather didn't like trousers of any sort on women. But the femininity of the shirt, both in fabric and style, counterbalanced the boyishness of the breeches. And what could be more traditionally seductive than a pair of black-stockinged ankles?

When she joined the men in the drawing-room, her grandfather was wearing a burgundy velvet smoking-jacket with a foulard cravat in the open collar of a silk shirt.

Roderick had changed into a well-cut suit of lightweight grey worsted. His shirt had blue and

white stripes with a plain white collar, and his tie
was dark blue silk. His hair was still slightly damp
from the shower, and the darkness of his beard was
less noticeable, suggesting that he had shaved.
Polished soft black leather loafers had replaced the
brown ones in which he had arrived.

They were both holding the elaborately cut glasses
Abel preferred to plain ones. His was a tumbler
containing brandy and soda. Roderick's was a glass
of pale sherry.

Her grandfather didn't ask her what she would
like to drink. He had grown up in a world where
women waited on men, not the other way round.
If he had noticed that in some circles men attended
to women's comfort he had seen no reason to
change the habits of a lifetime.

Knowing this, she smiled at them both and went
to the lavishly stocked cocktail cabinet to fix herself
what would look like a pink gin but was actually
the Angostura bitters and tonic without the gin.

Flower enjoyed wine with her meals. She had
avoided drinking spirits since the night when, sev-
enteen and trying to appear sophisticated, she had
asked her date for a vodka and tonic. Later she had
found herself coping with a pass which would have
been easier to handle if her wits had not been addled
by what in retrospect she'd guessed had been two
double vodkas.

The lid of the cabinet was lined with mirror-glass
in which she could see the two men standing on the
old Persian rug in front of the log fire. She shot a
swift glance at Roderick and saw he was watching
her.

He was still watching when she turned round and strolled to the fireside, pretending not to know he was looking at her.

Her grandfather was holding forth on American foreign policy. Evidently he had decided to drop the subject of the lease for the time being.

Flower seated herself in one of the Anstruthers' Hepplewhite painted elbow chairs and, crossing her legs, gently swung one velvet-shod foot. The cut steel buckle, one of a pair she had found in a London antiques market and stitched on the slippers herself, glimmered in the rosy firelight and the subdued radiance given off by two silk-shaded lamps.

She was striving to appear very calm, very much at her ease. But inwardly she was excited; intensely aware of the tall assured figure with a glass in one hand and the other thrust into the pocket of his trousers.

'Are you interested in politics, Miss Dursley?' he enquired a minute or two later when the flow of Abel's opinions stopped while he swallowed some brandy.

'Not in the least,' she admitted.

Long ago she had given up the pretence of being more—or less—intelligent than she was, or of liking things she didn't like in the hope of pleasing the man of the moment. It was better to be true to oneself, she had found. Pretence was too much of an effort. It was never worth it.

He moved away from Abel towards her. 'What does interest you?'

'I can answer that in one word—clothes!' said her grandfather with a chuckle. 'She's got cupboards full of 'em. Enough clothes to stock a boutique, and half of them never worn, I shouldn't mind betting ... or only the once.'

Before she could refute this statement and answer the question for herself, Watson announced dinner. A little vexed, but hopeful that during the meal she could correct the impression that her only interest was her appearance, she put aside her glass of tonic and led the way to the dining-room.

The long polished D-ended table could seat thirty people. When they were alone she and her grandfather sat together at one end of it. Earlier tonight she had given instructions to Watson that this arrangement should not be changed but that Roderick Anstruther should sit in her usual place, on her grandfather's right, facing the painting which looked like a portrait of him in fancy dress.

Usually it was the footman on duty who drew out and pushed in her chair. But tonight it was their guest who performed this courtesy.

'Thank you.' She flashed a smile at him before he walked round to his own place opposite hers.

As she shook out her napkin she wanted to say, 'It must be a very strange feeling for you to be here after such a long absence.' But she thought it wiser not to make any remark which might revive Abel's ire about the lease.

Instead she said, 'What is your opinion of American food? I found it rather good...especially the seafood.'

'The seafood and steaks are excellent, and the food served in private houses is often superb. But, like the British, as a nation they eat a lot of junk food.'

'Junk food? What d'you mean by that?' asked Abel.

'All the things people in the Western World eat which don't do them any good and probably do them great harm.'

Her grandfather grunted. 'Food is food as far as I'm concerned. There's nothing to beat good plain English food, in my opinion. I've no time for fancy foreign dishes smothered in sauce so you can't tell whether the meat or fish is fresh or not. I don't hold with dieting neither. Flower's always half starving herself... fasting... living on fruit juice. I believe in three meals a day. I'll be sixty-eight soon, but there's nothing wrong with my digestion. I've as good an appetite as you. Always have had. Couldn't have worked as hard as I have all my life if I hadn't eaten well.'

Usually, when her grandfather told people his age in that tone, they felt obliged to express some astonishment that he should be as old as he claimed. Roderick Anstruther said nothing. His eyes skimmed his host's ruddy jowls and the paunch straining the buttons of the smoking-jacket. Then he looked at Flower and said, 'Do you have a weight problem, Miss Dursley? I shouldn't have suspected it.'

'No, of course she doesn't,' said Abel. 'But you know what these modern girls are. They're all hell-bent on being as skinny as the models in fashion magazines. I keep telling her, any man who *is* a man, and not a pansy, like most of these designers, likes a girl with a bit of flesh on her. There's no pleasure in cuddling a bunch of matchsticks. Isn't that right?'

'There's certainly a happy medium between too much flesh and too little. I should have thought your granddaughter was an excellent example of it,' said his guest.

The odd thing was that although, presumably, this reply was intended as a compliment, it didn't sound like one. There was something too judicial about it, and the glance he gave at what he could see of Flower's figure was impersonal rather than personal.

However she decided to take it as a compliment. 'Thank you,' she said, smiling at him. 'Dodo exaggerates. I don't starve myself. Occasionally, after a lot of parties, I have one day on nothing but fruit juice. Otherwise I eat what I like.'

'And you like wholemeal bread, I notice,' he said, looking at the roll she had taken from the silver basket handed to them by the footman.

He had chosen a similar roll, but her grandfather, who had false teeth, had taken a crustless white roll made in his bread factory.

She said, 'Yes, I bought these in London this morning from a shop near my flat. I usually bring some back and they're kept in the fridge and then lightly damped and reheated. It makes them taste fresh from the oven. They're good, aren't they?' she finished, popping a piece into her mouth.

'Very good.' He turned to the old man. 'But isn't it *lèse-majesté* for your granddaughter to prefer these rolls to your products, Mr Dursley?'

The remark was made with a smile, but the tone and the glint in his eyes was somewhat sardonic.

'I don't know about that,' said Abel, 'but it seems a damned waste of money to be bringing bread from London when you can order whatever you want from the works, Flower. What's so special about that stuff? Apart from a fancy London price?'

Although he would have thought nothing of giving her a four-figure cheque—in addition to her generous allowance—to buy herself the latest thing in furs, had she worn furs—which she did not—he was oddly tight-fisted in small ways. He would spend several thousand pounds on a party to impress his cronies, yet grudge a few pence spent on other things.

'I think it tastes better than white bread, and it's more filling,' she answered. 'I like it even better than French bread.'

The younger man said, 'As a man of the people, Mr Dursley, doesn't it ever worry you that the people's "staff of life", as it used to be called, is now an inferior product to the bread of, say, a hundred years ago?'

'There's nothing inferior about my bread,' said Abel with a sharp glance at him. 'It's made in the most hygienic bakeries in the country, and it's sliced and wrapped to reach the housewife in perfect condition, ready to stick in the toaster and make into sandwiches or whatever way she wants to use it. You don't know who's handled those rolls you're eating. They could have goodness knows what germs on them.'

'True, but they're not germs which are likely to kill us and, if we had to, we could live on this for some time. A man wouldn't last very long on a regime of white bread and water,' his guest said drily. 'But perhaps it doesn't concern you that children brought up on white bread are being deprived of important nutrients?'

'Pah! Talking through your hat!' was Abel's impatient response. 'The children of this generation are a damn sight better fed than mine was, let me tell you. When I was a kid there was still plenty of rickets about. I've gone to bed hungry myself when my dad was out of work. There's none of that now. The kids of this country are better fed than they've ever been. Only the other week I was asked to present the prizes at a village school near here. They were kiddies from a housing estate, most of 'em, and as plump and healthy as my two lovely little great-grandchildren.'

'Plump children aren't necessarily healthy. They merely have different deficiencies from the children of your generation; deficiencies which may not surface until middle age.'

Roderick Anstruther spoke with a quiet authority quite different from Abel's dogmatism.

'I'm sure you know the history of your industry,' he went on. 'Commercial bread has been virtually valueless as food since the machinery to refine flour was invented. It's now so refined it has no goodness left in it.'

Seeing her grandfather's scowl growing darker, and feeling it was a contentious topic for their guest to have raised in the house of a bread-manufacturer, Flower said, rather stiffly, 'How do you know all this?'

'One of my father's friends is a leading American paediatrician who has retired to Arizona. He is seriously concerned by the increase in the number of overweight children, many of whom are actually undernourished in spite of being fat.'

To her relief, he then changed the subject by saying, 'You mentioned your flat in London. You work there, I take it, and come home at weekends?'

'No, I live here,' she answered. 'The flat is a *pied-à-terre* for when I have things to do in London. My work is here...running the house for my grandfather.'

As she saw him lifting one eyebrow, she added defensively, 'A large house doesn't run itself, and we do a lot of entertaining.'

'You must if it's a full-time job in spite of the staff you have here now.' His tone was undisguisedly sardonic. 'My mother used to manage with two or three part-time cleaners, but we lived very informally. Except on special occasions, we only used the library and the morning-room.'

'I reckon a place this size needs a staff of at least fifteen if it's to be kept as it should be,' said Abel.

'You may be right, although my mother used to say that, if a house is reasonably tidy and the flowers are well done, people don't notice dust.'

Their guest's glance came to rest briefly on the two dozen dark red roses in a modern silver bowl bought by Abel when he had discovered that all the containers in Lady Anstruther's flower-room were old soup tureens, teapots, jugs and mugs, many of them cracked or chipped. That they were lovely examples of Wedgwood creamware, Coalport and Worcester porcelains and other fine early china meant nothing to him. He had no use for anything damaged, however beautiful.

Nor, if they were like the flowers done by Emily Fairchild and her mother, would he have admired Lady Anstruther's arrangements of mixed garden and wild flowers. Knowing his preference for hot-house roses and orchids, Flower kept the hedgerow posies picked on her solitary walks to the small sitting-room adjoining her bedroom.

'You surprise me,' Abel said acidly. 'One thing I admired about *my* mother, God bless her, was the

way she kept her home spotless. She went through
some hard times, poor soul, but she never lowered
her standards. You could have eaten your dinner
off her kitchen floor.'

To Flower it was plain that, by implying that
Lady Anstruther, for all her blue blood, had been
a slattern compared to the late Florrie Dursley, her
grandfather was getting his own back for their visitor's condemnation of the bread produced at the
works.

She could see that, apart from being at loggerheads over the lease, the two men were at odds in
every way. All their values were completely different. They would never get on with each other.

Which was going to make it awkward for her if
the man on the other side of the table was the one
she had been waiting for so long.

The first course was followed by Abel's favourite
sirloin. It was roasted on the bone and accompanied by Yorkshire pudding, creamed swedes,
cabbage, roast potatoes, a thickened gravy and
horse-radish sauce.

Flower found herself watching Roderick
Anstruther's hands as they cut the prime Scottish
beef. She had always had a thing about hands.
However attractive a man might be facially, his
looks made no impression on her if there was
something offputting about his hands.

However she could find no fault with their guest's
hands. The long lean fingers were rather square at
the tips, with neatly pared, very clean nails. His
hands were as brown as his face. Perhaps he had
picked up his tan while arranging his father's fu-
neral in Arizona, or perhaps even in New York it

was possible for someone with his colouring to tan during summer lunch-hours and after work. Although, if he had to supplement his income with a second job, it didn't sound as if he had much time to relax.

She wondered what the jobs were, and was going to ask him, when he started questioning her grandfather about some changes he had noticed locally. Relieved that the conversation had taken a less acrimonious turn, she reserved her questions for later on.

The beef was followed by an apple pie with Cornish cream, after which the butler served English cheeses. Flower and their guest sat out this course, although he let her grandfather press him to try the vintage port Abel liked to drink with his Stilton.

'We'll have coffee in the library, Watson,' he ordered.

'Very good, sir.'

'I've made some changes in the library... brought it up to date,' said Abel, piling cheese on a water biscuit.

The younger man's eyes narrowed slightly. 'Oh, really? In what way?'

'I've had all the shabby old chairs put away in one of the attics and installed some decent new seating. It's an entertainments centre now, with projection TV as well as video and a first-class stereo-system.'

To Flower's secret embarrassment, he then announced what he had spent on each piece of equipment.

'When we don't have company we spend most evenings watching a film or two,' he went on. 'We'll watch one tonight if you like.'

Her heart sank. Her grandfather's favourite movies were slapstick comedies with Laurel and Hardy or Abbott and Costello. He would screen them not once but repeatedly, guffawing as much at the third or fourth showing as at the first, while she, by the light of a reading lamp, would lose herself in a book.

She had been a bookworm all her life. Books had been her refuge, her solace, her escape from loneliness. Her grandfather didn't know it because it was a long time since he had been there, but her flat in London was crowded with books, not just new ones but old ones as well. The hundreds of volumes in the Anstruthers' library had given her a liking for the look of tooled-leather bindings and the feel and smell of old paper.

No one whose impression of her had been formed by reading about her in the gossip columns would have suspected that six nights out of seven she was to be found, not at a wild party in London, but tucked up in bed with a book.

In her nineteenth year, when unhappiness had made her reckless about whom she was seen with and where, she had had the misfortune to be spotlighted by the gossip writers. Exaggerated accounts of her activities had been appearing ever since. Tagged as 'blonde playgirl Flower Dursley', she had found it impossible to shed a reputation which, if not entirely without foundation, was ninety-five-per-cent myth.

If Sir Roderick thought the library had been ruined by having the centre refurnished with a U-

shaped sectional sofa surrounding a huge white fur
rug on which stood three dark glass coffee-tables,
he did not show any reaction at finding Abel's idea
of *grand luxe* set down in the middle of a fine
eighteenth-century book-room.

He seemed genuinely interested in the video
equipment, and listened attentively to his host's explanation of its finer points.

When they settled down to watch the film he had
selected, her grandfather occupied his usual place
in the centre of the U with the other two flanking
him on the curved sections.

Roderick Anstruther refused Abel's offer of a
liqueur and cigar with his coffee. He sat with his
long legs crossed and his jacket unbuttoned to show
a black leather belt, with a rectangular silver buckle,
slotted through the loops of his trousers.

Flower had noticed many such buckles, usually
monogrammed, worn by the rich Americans they
had met while staying at Palm Beach. She had had
one monogrammed for her brother. But she wasn't
sure that he liked it, and if he continued to put on
weight the belt would need replacing with a longer
one. Stephen's body was not hard and fit like that
of the man sitting on the far side of her grandfather, waiting for the film to begin.

With a guest present she felt obliged to watch it.
The star was one of the idols of her grandfather's
youth, a toothy ukulele-playing Lancashire com-
edian called George Formby. Some of his songs
were catchy, but Flower thought the script was terrible—terrible enough to be funny.

Her sense of humour was never far below the
surface and she found herself unexpectedly amused
and at times rather touched by the naïveté of the

film. From occasional glances at him, she judged
that their guest was not as bored as she had feared
he would be. Amusement took away the hard, un-
compromising expression of his face in repose. She
liked his low-pitched chuckle.

She had hoped that tonight her grandfather
would be content with one film, leaving the rest of
the evening free for conversation. Sometimes he
went to bed early and watched television there. She
would have liked very much to have their guest to
herself, both in order to get to know him better and
to show him that she was not quite as Dodo had
presented her.

However, to her dismay, as soon as the Formby
movie ended Abel said, 'We'll have a documentary
next. I think you'll find this quite an eye-opener.'
He turned to her. 'You haven't seen this one yet,
Flower.'

The film which followed was about the mill and
the factories. Embroidered with facts and figures
to give it the air of an impartial study, it was basi-
cally an advertisement for Abel's products.

He, very naturally, watched it with a beam of
pride. But Flower saw that their visitor was staring
at the screen under brows drawn into a frown. She
could tell by the flicker of a muscle at his jaw that
his teeth were clenched with suppressed anger. The
strength of his reaction baffled her.

Why should it make him furious to see the white-
uniformed employees, busy operating the complex
machinery, relaxing in the staff cafeteria and, in
the case of the women, collecting their toddlers
from the crêche at the end of their shifts?

As Abel had said during dinner, not only his
bread but all his products—which ranged from

sausages to television suppers, ready to re-heat by
microwave, and baby foods—were manufactured
in model conditions. She knew from her own visits
to the factories that they were as clean, bright and
efficient as the film depicted.

Could it be merely that he resented being shown
the background to her grandfather's fortune? The
fortune which had, in a sense, ousted his parents
from their rightful place in the world?

No, she couldn't believe it was that. There was
something much more complex behind his
glowering reaction to the scenes flashing on the large
screen.

'Impressive, eh?' Abel remarked after the film
had ended by showing actors purporting to be three
generations of a family sitting down to have Sunday
tea round a table laden with his foodstuffs.

Afterwards Flower wasn't sure what prompted
her to launch into an enthusiastic encomium of the
film's merits. She thought it must be because her
intuition told her that any comment their guest
might make was liable to give Abel apoplexy.

Though she knew little about him, her instinct
told her that Roderick Anstruther was no hyp-
ocrite. It would be impossible for him, having
watched the film with that fierce expression on his
face, to offer the sort of unctuous comment her
grandfather expected.

So she got in ahead of him, saying brightly, 'It's
terrific, Dodo. I didn't know you were having a film
made. It's very well done. Those children in the
final shots are a great improvement on the two little
horrors stuffing themselves in your last TV
commercial.'

She was rattling on in the same vein when, to her relief, Watson entered.

'Mr Dursley is on the telephone, sir.'

Abel picked up the cordless telephone which went everywhere with him and, in a tone of considerable annoyance, said, 'What the hell's gone wrong now, Steve?'

Flower could hear her brother's voice, but not what he was saying.

After a few moments her grandfather interrupted him. 'Hold on a minute.' To the others, he added, 'I'll take this call in the study.'

'That was my brother,' Flower explained after he had stumped out of the room. 'Have you any brothers or sisters, Sir Roderick?'

He shook his head, moving from the section where he had been sitting to one closer to hers. 'No, I haven't. Why not call me Roderick? May I use your first name?'

'Of course. Tell me, what *are* your plans for this house? Do you want to live here yourself? Or is there something about us which makes us unacceptable tenants?'

'As I've only just met you and your grandfather, it could hardly be a personal antipathy, could it?' was his equable reply.

'I don't know,' she said with a gesture signifying puzzlement. 'Perhaps your father regretted leasing the house and charged you with the task of getting rid of us.'

'On the contrary, my father often said he wished he had moved to Arizona sooner. He liked the American way of life. He was a younger son. It was his elder brother who should have inherited the place, but he was killed in the Second World War.

My mother liked America too. We all did. But now my parents are dead I no longer have family ties there and, as I was telling your grandfather earlier, this house is entailed. It's mine now, but not to sell. I have to keep it for my son, if I have one.'

He paused, looking at her thoughtfully, before he went on, 'The nine months till the present lease ends should be ample time for your grandfather to find somewhere else to live. Shall you mind leaving here? Wouldn't you be equally if not more comfortable in a large modern house?'

The honest answer would have been, 'No, I love this house now. It's been my home since I was ten. I can't bear the idea of leaving it.'

But if she said that it could only make him uncomfortable, and she didn't want to do that.

It was his right to come back. In spite of his time in America, he belonged here as they never had. Her grandfather would fight him if the option he held gave him a chance of winning. But Flower knew that, deep in her heart and absurd as it might seem to anyone else, she was not on her grandfather's side. She wanted Roderick Anstruther to have possession of his ancestral home.

Aloud, she said, 'I shouldn't like to live in a new house. I don't think much of contemporary domestic architecture—or indeed any modern architecture. My brother has an ultra-modern house, designed for him and my sister-in-law by a prizewinning architect, but I don't like it at all. How long are you staying in England?'

'For two weeks. There are various people in London I want to look up. Will you be there again in the next fortnight?'

'Probably. I'm there most weeks for a night or two.'

'Perhaps we could have dinner together?'

'I'd like to.'

The smile in her grey eyes was a tacit admission that she found him attractive and wanted to see more of him, no matter what the situation was between him and her grandfather.

It was a long time since she had smiled at a man with open warmth. Mostly she played it cool, letting them make all the running.

But Roderick was not like a stranger. He was the embodiment of someone who had been her *beau idéal* for years, just as Andrew Fairchild had always personified Emily's ideal man.

'I don't know which are the best places to eat nowadays. You will have to advise me,' he said.

Flower, who had dined at all the fashionable restaurants too often to be excited by them, and who knew how expensive they were even if she never paid the bills, said, 'Why not come and eat at my flat?'

It was not an invitation she would normally have issued on so short an acquaintance. In fact he was the first man she had ever asked to dine alone with her there. The indiscretions of her nineteenth year were a thing of the past. She was much more circumspect now, even if the columnists would not have it so.

Seeing the slight lift of his right eyebrow, she wondered if she had given him the wrong impression. But, before she could hasten to correct it by adding that she had some friends she thought he would enjoy meeting, her grandfather returned.

Abel had not been reared on the belief that dirty linen should never be washed in public. He said what he thought, when he thought it, regardless of any embarrassment caused to his hearers.

Now, in spite of Roderick's presence, he said crossly, 'That damn fool brother of yours seems incapable of putting a foot right. Heaven knows what'll happen if I leave him in charge when I pass on. Call Watson. I need a drink. What about you?' This to Roderick.

'No, thank you. If you'll excuse me I'll go to bed.'

Abel nodded. 'Right you are. Tomorrow I'll be busy in the morning, but Flower will show you round and look after you. We'll discuss the lease after lunch.'

After Roderick had left them, he went on, 'I'm beginning to think it's a pity I didn't take you into the business instead of Steve. I don't hold with girls having jobs, except as something to keep them out of mischief until they get married. But, as you don't seem to want a husband, I might have done worse than train you up to take over.'

'I'm not cut out for management, Dodo. And I *should* like a husband, if I could find one to suit me.'

'Seems to me there've been half a dozen who would have suited you. I don't think you know what you do want,' he retorted irritably, his brimming annoyance with Stephen spilling over on to her.

'Well, don't let it worry you, darling. I'm not quite on the shelf yet, you know,' she said, trying to tease away his glower.

'Maybe not, but I'd like to see you settled. Where the devil is Watson?'

'He's off duty now. I'll get your drink. What would you like? Brandy and soda?'

He nodded. 'What were you and that fellow talking about while I was out of the room?'

'Nothing special. Just chit-chat.'

'I noticed he'd moved to sit nearer. Was he chatting you up?'

She shook her head. She didn't want to discuss Roderick with her grandfather, who regarded every man she dated either as a possible fortune-hunter or a prospective husband.

At the beginning of something which might turn out to be an important relationship, or nothing more than an acquaintance, she didn't think ahead to the outcome. She knew what she felt at this moment—that she might be on the brink of a wonderful, life-changing experience. But, with only a fortnight in hand before Roderick returned to America, maybe nothing would come of it.

But when she tried to steer the conversation away from their unexpected house guest Abel was not to be deflected.

He said, 'He's got a few bees in his bonnet, judging by his talk at dinner, but he's a fine-looking fellow. You could do a lot worse for yourself...and it would solve a lot of problems.'

'Dodo, are you seriously suggesting that I should set my cap at him to save us the trouble of finding somewhere else to live?' she asked with some exasperation.

CHAPTER THREE

'CERTAINLY not! You've no need to set your cap at any man. You're a beautiful girl with a lot of money behind you. You can take your pick,' Abel said complacently.

'Not entirely,' was Flower's dry reply. 'There are men who look for other things besides looks and money.'

'Such as?'

'Intelligence...character...breeding. I'm not and never can be well-bred. Roderick would never marry beneath him.'

Abel's face purpled angrily. 'Beneath him! Don't talk piffle, girl. You're as good as he is any day.'

She shrugged her slim shoulders. 'I'm not his social equal, Dodo. And, with only very rare exceptions, the aristocracy marry each other, not outsiders.'

'You're not an outsider,' he thundered. 'I sent you to one of the most exclusive schools in England, and to a posh finishing-school. There's no difference between you and a duke's daughter that I can see.'

'On the surface, not very much. But I'm not a member of the charmed circle. My grandmother didn't "come out" with their grandmothers. My brother didn't go to Eton with their brothers. My forebears were their forebears' servants. We are *nouveau riche*, Dodo, and the fact that Emily's parents didn't discourage *her* from being my friend

46

doesn't mean they wouldn't have discouraged her brothers from taking an interest in me if they had been closer to my age.'

Abel fumed but said nothing. She could see his mind searching for a way to demolish her case. In a few moments he found it.

'What about when some duke or other married that American heiress ... one of the Vanderbilts?' he countered.

'That was one of the rare exceptions and it was a disastrous marriage. They had nothing in common and were miserable with each other. Surely you don't want me to contract an unhappy marriage merely to have a title, do you?'

'No, no, I didn't suggest that. I may have a title myself before I've done,' he told her with a covetous gleam in his eyes. 'But you've just admitted you'd like a husband, and it strikes me you could do worse than consider young Anstruther. As for him not thinking you good enough, that's stuff and nonsense. I'm not sure yet what his game is in trying to shift us, but I've a shrewd idea his dad won't have left him more than a few thousand. Without money he's no catch for a girl, and most of your so-called upper crust aren't as well-heeled as they used to be.'

'As far as I'm concerned, the primary requisite for marriage is love,' she said firmly. 'I'm going to bed now. I was up late last night and I need to catch up my sleep.'

She bade him good night and went up to her beautiful bedroom, which would have been even more beautiful had he not installed the showbiz bed in place of the original four-poster with its ice-blue silk curtains to match those at the two tall windows.

The carpet was ice-blue and gold, and the floor-boards beneath it creaked in places as she moved about, putting away her clothes and thinking over the disturbing conversation downstairs.

By conceiving the idea of a match between herself and Roderick, her grandfather had forced her to face things she wasn't ready to face yet and would have preferred to ignore.

What he didn't realise, she thought ruefully, was that he himself, with his brash ways and uncouth manners, was a major obstacle between her and a marriage into the aristocracy. They might, at a pinch, find her acceptable. But Abel—never. From her point of view it was a case of love me, love my grandfather. She might have mixed feelings about him, but she wouldn't stand for a husband or in-laws looking down on him.

Actually she didn't think Roderick did look down on the old man in the social sense. She felt he disliked him for another reason; what it was she couldn't yet fathom.

In spite of having said that she wanted an early night, she wasn't in the least sleepy. She decided to write to tell Emily about the man now asleep in the room which had been his as a boy.

There was a half-written letter to her friend on one of the disks she kept in a box by her personal computer in the adjoining sitting-room. She had bought it and taught herself to use it for the same reason that she had taken a crash-course in French. She liked to feel that, in the unlikely event that it ever became necessary for her to work, she had some qualifications for earning a living.

A few minutes later, with what she had already written displayed on the monitor screen, she con-

tinued the letter by describing her time in London
and the clothes she had bought. Emily's interest in
clothes had not diminished because she was married
to the son of a landowner and now spent much of
her time in the serviceable garments suitable for her
life as the wife of a working farmer and the mother
of a year-old daughter.

Having dealt with her London news, Flower then
went on to describe coming home and finding
Roderick in the house.

> I'm not sure what to make of him yet. One
> wouldn't describe him as reserved, but nor is he
> the outgoing type. I feel he's rather like an
> iceberg. There's a lot more under the surface than
> is visible at first sight, and a collision with him
> could be dangerous.

Having brought the letter up to date, she tapped
the keys which would keep it stored in the computer's memory until she had some more to add.
Then she switched off the machine, covered it with
an Indian silk shawl to protect it from dust and
hide it—it was useful but a terrible eyesore—and
set about taking off her make-up and brushing her
teeth.

After that she read for a while before setting the
alarm which would wake her with music at seven-
thirty and, finally, switching off the light.

But at midnight she was still awake, unable to
stop thinking about Roderick and the changes he
might bring to their lives

It was a full moon; a brilliant night. Restless, she
slipped out of bed and went to the window to look
down at the garden, where tomorrow she might get
to know him better.

The house was built in two wings at right angles to each other. To her surprise she saw lights on in the morning-room.

She was wondering if one of the staff could have left them on by mistake, when she remembered Roderick saying that, in his parents' time, they had used the library and morning-room more than any of the other ground-floor rooms. She felt sure he was down there now, his sleep pattern disrupted by being in a different time zone from the one he had inhabited the night before.

Suddenly she couldn't wait until tomorrow to talk to him again. Flicking on a light, she chose a housecoat of dark red panné velvet to cover her transparent nightie. Quickly she brushed her hair and ran a stick of colourless gloss over what a man had once called her Botticelli lips, presumably because of their sweeping curves.

The moon lit her way along the corridor and down the wide staircase. Some of the rooms downstairs were locked up last thing at night as a precaution against burglars. The exterior of the house was protected by a sophisticated alarm system. In the unlikely event of a thief breaking in, he would find it difficult to pass from one room to another. But the morning-room contained none of the valuable paintings and clocks the Anstruthers had left behind them.

For a moment before she opened the door she hesitated outside it, wondering if she might be intruding on reminiscences of his youth which Roderick would prefer to dwell on in private.

However, having reached this point, she was not inclined to retreat without at least speaking to him.

If she sensed that he wanted to be left alone, she would withdraw.

Hoping her entrance wouldn't startle him too much when he thought he was the only person about, she turned the handle and walked in.

He was sitting in a chair facing the door, wearing a dark brown silk dressing-gown over pale grey pyjamas. These were not silk. The material looked like poplin, and perhaps he was only wearing the trousers as she couldn't see any sign of a jacket.

On his lap was a large leather-bound book she recognised as one of several albums of family photographs from the highest of a bank of shelves containing bound volumes of magazines such as *Punch*, *Country Life* and *London Illustrated News*.

Visitors' books, dating back to the last century, and novels and biographies from the twenties and thirties were also housed on the shelves.

At the sight of her he closed the album and rose. Obviously he had very steady nerves. She would have jumped out of her skin if anyone had walked in on her at that hour. He didn't seem even surprised.

'Please don't get up. I saw the light from my room and thought it must have been left on by mistake. Can't you sleep? I suppose in New York it's early evening.'

'Yes, and I don't usually go to bed much before midnight. You're also a night-bird, I gather?'

His vivid eyes appraised her velvet robe which, although it had a scarf collar and the hem swept the floor, clung to the contours of her body, the flattened pile catching the light to accentuate the curves of her breasts and hips.

She sat down on the chintz-covered sofa. 'I go to bed early but read late. Tonight I was finishing a novel, and then I got up to look at the garden by moonlight, which is when I noticed the light on down here.'

'You're not nervous of wandering about the house at night?'

Flower shook her head. 'Should I be? Is it supposed to be haunted? We've never heard that.'

'There are no family ghosts . . . no grey ladies or headless Elizabethans. Most of my forebears died peacefully in bed.'

'Piers Anstruther died a violent death, although not here,' she reminded him.

'Piers? Oh, yes, the chap in the dining-room. How did you find out about him?'

'He's mentioned in some of the books about the English Civil War in the library. One can't help becoming interested in a man whose portrait one sees every day. If you were to grow a moustache and wear your hair long you'd look very like him.'

'So my mother used to tell me.'

He had resumed his seat and crossed his long legs. His bare ankles were brown. He was wearing needlepoint slippers, dark brown with an almost invisible monogram in navy or black—it was difficult to tell in artificial light—on the fronts.

She wondered who had worked them for him. His mother? Or one of his girlfriends?

In England, dressing-gowns like his came from the elegant men's shops in Jermyn Street in London and were very expensive. Which didn't mean that it couldn't have been a present from his parents because, however hard up they were, people like the

Anstruthers bought very good things and wore them until they disintegrated.

It might even have belonged to his father. Emily's brothers wore clothes which had belonged to their grandfather. Good tweeds and handmade shoes almost never wore out, and the country houses of England were full of the relics of earlier generations which, from time to time, came back into fashion.

These thoughts flashed through Flower's mind in a matter of seconds and, with no noticeable hiatus in the conversation, she said, 'Apart from Piers, and your father and uncle, who both fought in the last war, most of your ancestors seem to have enjoyed doing nothing. You mentioned having two jobs. What kind of jobs are they?'

'I'm what is known in America as a cardiologist—a physician specialising in diseases of the heart,' he answered. 'Many young doctors over there have to go in for moonlighting during the years between qualifying and becoming consultants. It's a bad system because half the time they're asleep on their feet. But it's the way things are. Fortunately, I've passed that stage of my career now.'

The discovery that he was a doctor surprised her. A medical career had not been among her speculations about his means of making a living.

'Was it your mother's illness which influenced you to take up medicine?' she asked.

'It was a factor in my choice. She'd been ill since I was about thirteen. Not with heart trouble. She had a lung condition. Seeing at first hand how illness blights people's lives made medicine seem a worthwhile occupation.'

'But if you come back to this country will you be allowed to practise here? And surely English doctors earn much less than their American counterparts? I thought that was why some of our doctors have left here to work over there.'

'True, but here I have one big advantage—this house and its grounds. I want to establish a clinic. This place, being within easy reach of London, is ideally situated.'

'I see. Why didn't you tell my grandfather this?'

'Your grandfather seems to prefer jumping to conclusions and telling people what they can or can't do to asking questions and listening to the answers,' was his sardonic reply.

'You don't like him, do you?' she said bluntly.

'I like his granddaughter.'

He left the chair and came to sit beside her on the sofa. 'I'd been told you were a stunning-looking girl, but I hadn't expected you to be quite such a knock-out.'

Accustomed as she was to handling, with aplomb, every kind of male approach, Flower was inwardly taken aback by this swift change of pace from ordinary conversation to a flirtation.

'Been told? By whom?' she enquired, aware that her pulse had quickened.

'By people who had seen you at places like Annabel's and knew you were living in our house. One doesn't lose touch because one lives overseas.'

He had turned his body towards her, one arm stretched along the back of the sofa, the other hand thrust in the pocket of his robe.

She knew that any minute now he was going to kiss her, and it made her as trembly inside as if she had never been kissed before.

Roderick removed his hand from his pocket and took told of her chin, turning her face towards him while at the same time his arm left the back of the sofa and encircled her shoulders.

At close quarters he seemed even bigger than he did at a distance, the formidable breadth of his shoulders making her feel slight and fragile.

His mouth touched hers, lightly and gently, and yet there was nothing tentative in the firm way he drew her against him. She had a strange feeling, as if they had done this before and he was no stranger but someone she had known forever. She yielded, her soft lips quivering and parting as the kiss changed, becoming more ardent.

It was quite a long time, several months, since anyone had embraced her. She had almost forgotten how it felt to be held by a muscular arm with a warm male hand on her throat, tilting her head back.

One kiss merged with another... and another. A small voice at the back of her mind advised her to call a halt before things got out of hand. But somehow she hadn't the power to bring an end to a kiss like no other she had ever experienced.

Even when his hand slipped inside the red velvet robe and caressed her breast through the flimsy stuff of her nightgown she did not immediately resist.

It was only when, moments later, she grasped that he had every intention of making love to her there and then on the sofa that she started to struggle to free herself.

Wrenching her mouth away, she gasped, 'No... please... stop... This is crazy.'

'What's crazy about it? I want you—and you want me,' he said huskily.

His blue eyes were brilliant with desire as they feasted on the golden skin revealed by her disordered clothing.

The robe was wide open now, and one shoulder-tie of her nightie had been swiftly and deftly undone to remove the last flimsy barrier between her throbbing flesh and his palm. One long slender leg was bare to the top of her thigh.

She stared, aghast, at her dishevelment. But her frantic efforts to cover herself were frustrated when he caught her by the wrists, saying mockingly, 'Don't be shy. I am a doctor, remember.'

'Let me go! Please... *please* ... let me go.'

She tried to break free but couldn't. His fingers were steely, enclosing her wrists not tightly but as inescapably as handcuffs.

'You don't really want me to stop now,' he told her caressingly.

She realised it was useless to argue with him. He was too strongly aroused to listen to belated protests.

Forcing herself to relax, she whispered, 'You're hurting me, Roderick.'

He wasn't, but her sudden surrender was enough to make him let go and start to caress her again.

For an instant or two she submitted. Then with all her strength she gave him one violent push and sprang up and ran.

She didn't stop running until she reached her bedroom, where she slammed the door behind her and locked it before she stumbled to a chair. She collapsed in it, panting and shaking.

Halfway up the stairs she had known that he wasn't coming after her. If he had given chase he would have caught her. Nor did she really believe that there had been any serious danger of his taking her by force. He wasn't that kind of man.

He had merely assumed, and not entirely without reason, that she was the kind of girl who, on the strength of attraction at sight, would be willing to let him make love to her.

There were girls like that. She knew some. But she wasn't one of them. Love for her was no casual pleasure, no automatic sequel to dinner *à deux* or an evening spent dancing at Annabel's.

The folly of having allowed him to go as far as he had was something she could never explain to him. He would see her behaviour as that of a deliberate tease who on this occasion had miscalculated and left it almost too late to escape the consequences of her stupid pastime.

Not that he himself had acted creditably. The seduction of any female who showed herself at all willing might be forgivable in the case of a medical student, but it wasn't what most people expected of a qualified physician of his age. Clearly, Roderick Anstruther was an unashamed and ruthless womaniser who never missed an opportunity to add another scalp to his belt.

It was almost four in the morning before Flower finally slept. Until then she tossed and turned, unable to rid her mind of the embarrassment of having to face him at breakfast tomorrow, or to quieten the physical reactions stirred up by his caresses.

Try as she would, she couldn't stop herself thinking about what it would be like to be in bed with him.

Well, if she really wanted to know, it would be only too easy to find out, she told herself crossly.

At the flat she could do as she pleased; have a different lover every week if she felt like it. After all, she was nearly twenty-three. Who was she saving herself for if not for this blue-eyed giant who, in his person if not his nature, represented all that she found attractive in a man?

It might be an excellent idea to get both him and his ancestor out of her system forever in a rip-roaring two-week affair which would end when he went back to America.

The alarm woke her out of a deep sleep, and Flower knew at once that something catastrophic had happened but not, for some seconds, what it was.

As memory came back she groaned. How could she have made such a fool of herself?

Part of the reason Roderick had made such a heavy pass at her had probably been because of her invitation to dine at her flat without any mention of other guests. She ought to have clarified that earlier.

On the other hand, it seemed likely that, on the strength of hearsay, he had already decided she was easily beddable before he had even laid eyes on her. She wondered who had told him about her, and what they had said.

She felt tired till she'd had a shower. But a few minutes under the jet of warm water washed away her fatigue and restored her normal vitality. Probably because she didn't drink, she had always been able to survive a short night without feeling a wreck the next day.

She dressed in slim-fitting grey trousers and a grey cashmere sweater with a collar of old lace. On her left wrist, as well as her watch, she always wore three gold bangles: one a present from Andrew Fairchild when she had been a bridesmaid at his wedding, another a present from Stephen for her eighteenth birthday, and a third which Dodo had bought her at the jewellery shop in the famous Breakers Hotel at Palm Beach when they had spent a winter holiday there.

She liked rings and had a collection, some found in London's antique markets, some on her travels. Today she chose four of her favourites and slipped them on her slender fingers. Her nails were filed level with her fingertips and painted with colourless varnish.

On the way downstairs she met John.

Smiling at him, she said, 'Good morning. I think our guest should be given a call or, having come from New York, he may oversleep.'

'Sir Roderick has been up for some time, miss. He went out for a run before breakfast. You'll find him in the dining-room with Mr Dursley.'

'Oh... I see. Thank you.' She passed on.

So he started the day with a run, did he? She wished Stephen would take more exercise. What with being many pounds overweight, and in a constant state of stress from trying, usually unsuccessfully, to fulfil their grandfather's expectations of him, her brother seemed a likely candidate for an early heart attack.

She found the two men eating kippers. Roderick rose from his chair as she gave him a cool, 'Good morning,' before bending to kiss her grandfather.

At breakfast Abel helped himself from the covered dish left on the sideboard, and he made his own toast. The toaster, on a long lead, stood within his reach on the table and he usually ate half a dozen slices, thickly spread with butter and marmalade.

Flower's normal breakfast consisted of orange juice, grapefruit and coffee. Abel drank tea, strong and sweet.

The men had been discussing the latest international news, which her grandfather had heard on an early bulletin on the radio while he was shaving. As they continued their conversation she filled her cup from the glass jug standing in readiness on its hot-plate.

As she sipped her orange juice she was conscious that nervousness was making her hand shake slightly. It vexed her to feel flustered when Roderick showed no sign of discomfiture.

She had swallowed three cups of coffee by the time her grandfather stood up and said to his guest, 'No need for you to hurry yourself, but I must be off. Flower will keep you company this morning, and this afternoon we'll get down to business. I'll see you at lunch.'

As soon as he had left the room, she said briskly, 'I'm sure you don't need a guided tour of your own home, and would probably prefer to wander about by yourself. As I have various things to do this morning I'll leave you to look around at your leisure.'

'Running away... again,' he said blandly.

In the act of rising, she checked. 'Not at all. I——'

'You're quite safe,' he interrupted. 'I got the message last night. ''Admire me. Desire me. But don't expect to go beyond the preliminaries.'' Right?'

Her face flamed. 'That isn't fair. I did nothing
to encourage you even to kiss me.'

'Apart from coming downstairs when everyone
else was in bed, every blonde hair in place and
wearing a garment calculated to raise any normal
male's blood-pressure. You'd been sending out encouraging signals all evening, my dear,' he informed her.

On the point of hotly denying it, she realised that
perhaps it was true.

Recovering her self-possession, she said coldly,
'It couldn't be, could it, that my grandfather isn't
the only one who jumps to conclusions? You said
you'd been told things about me. If one of them
was that I'm some sort of nymphomaniac, it doesn't
happen to be true. I won't deny that I found you
attractive—at first. But, since your extraordinary
demonstration that you *are* a lecher, I've revised
that opinion.'

Instead of being crushed by this riposte, he had
the effrontery to grin. 'I haven't revised mine of
you. I still think you're a ravishing girl, and it's
wasting time not to spend the morning in bed. But
it would raise the staff's eyebrows, I suppose, so if
you insist on postponing the inevitable for a few
days I'm prepared to go along with you.'

For ten seconds or more she was speechless.

'It is *not* inevitable!' she snapped. 'I have no intention of going to bed with you—ever!'

'If you say so.' His tone was sceptical. 'But I
think it's been inevitable since the moment we met.
You've already admitted to being attracted. I felt,
and still do, the same way.'

'But I don't,' she answered shortly. 'I detest men who take it for granted that every girl is a pushover. Now if you'll excuse me——'

She would have stalked out of the room, but he said, 'No, I won't excuse you. Your grandfather asked you to keep me company and I'm not prepared to be left to my own devices from now until lunchtime. Do you drink a lot of that!'—with a gesture at the coffee-maker.

Disconcerted by this abrupt change of subject, she said, 'I always have it for breakfast, and I suppose I drink four or five cups during the day.'

'You should try to break the addiction. Caffeine isn't good for anyone, and it's probably more dangerous for women than for men.'

'Why?'

'If they're pregnant it may have a bad effect on their babies, and it's also implicated in fibrocystic disease.'

'I don't know what that is.'

'Non-malignant lumps in the breasts. The elimination of caffeine has been shown to reverse their development.'

Although both his tone and his manner were now completely impersonal, his explanation was a reminder of his warm hands caressing her body the night before.

'I thought there was caffeine in tea too,' she said, hoping he wouldn't notice she was blushing again, although not as fierily as before.

'There is, but very weak tea made with milk is less harmful than strong black coffee. *Tisanes* are the best thing to drink.'

'Teas made with herbs? They sound horrible. Do you practise what you preach?'

'Not always in other people's houses. I do when I have any choice in the matter.'

They had risen and moved to the door which he opened for her as he said, 'Good health is something which most people take for granted until they lose it. But ill health is often self-inflicted. As well as cutting out coffee, you ought to eat a better breakfast.'

'I don't feel hungry in the morning.'

'You would if you got up earlier and ran round the garden a few times.'

'I'm not the athletic type. Where would you like to start the tour?'

'Outside, as it's such a fine morning. It'll be rather wet underfoot. We'd better wear boots—if there's a pair I can borrow.'

The butler had just emerged from the door leading to the staff quarters.

'Watson, have we a pair of wellingtons to fit Sir Roderick?' Flower asked him.

'What size, sir?'

'Eleven.'

'I'll see what we can do, sir.'

'Mine are upstairs. I shan't be long,' she said, leaving him in the hall.

Her waterproof boots were bright red, with a quilted gilet to match. With a silk scarf tied in an Ascot and a pair of warm woolly gloves, she was ready for what promised to be a difficult morning.

CHAPTER FOUR

WHEN Flower returned to the hall, Roderick was pulling on stout rubber boots.

'Won't you need your windcheater?' she asked, when he seemed prepared to go outside in his lightweight navy jersey.

'I don't think so. I rarely feel cold.'

'You were out before breakfast, I hear.'

'Yes, I'm hooked on aerobics. If I don't get my pre-breakfast "fix" I feel out of kilter all day. If you're not the athletic type, what type are you? What are you hooked on?'

'You've already been told that—clothes. I live for clothes,' she said flippantly as they left the warmth of the house for the crisp chill of the outer air.

There had been a frost in the night and the smooth lawns surrounding the house were still silver-grey in the shadows of the ancient cedars. Where the frost had thawed in the sun, the grass shimmered and sparkled.

'I don't believe that,' he said. 'I think you must have other interests. Do you ride?'

'No, I'm not the horsey type either. I just sit about reading *Vogue*, eating soft-centred chocolates and worrying about my nails.'

She had set off at a brisk pace along the path which led from the east front of the house to the yew-hedged Italian garden. But as she finished

speaking a hard hand fell on her shoulder, forcing
her to halt if she didn't want to topple backwards.

'If you're going to continue in that vein you may
find yourself reading *Vogue* standing up for a few
days,' he said mildly. 'Come down from your high
horse, Flower. If a girl I have only just met invites
me to dine at her flat it's not an unreasonable assumption that anything goes.'

Her grey eyes flashed with anger as she tried to
shrug free of the clamp-like grip on her shoulder.

'The unreasonable assumption was that you
would have been my only guest. I wasn't planning
a tête-à-tête. It was going to be a dinner party. But
I suppose that wouldn't have occurred to you, accustomed as you are to women falling like skittles
if you so much as glance at them.'

'You didn't say it would be a dinner party.'

'I didn't get time. Dodo came back before I could
go into details, and then you went to bed.'

'Am I to take it the invitation has been rescinded
now?'

'I'm surprised you have to ask.'

'What do you want? An apology?'

His blue eyes looked down into hers with an expression hard to interpret, but it didn't look like
contrition. That it wasn't was confirmed when he
went on, 'I'm afraid you're not going to get one.
I'm not going to say I'm sorry for something I enjoyed, and you enjoyed too—if you're honest.'

She lowered her lashes, finding it impossible to
hold that penetrating gaze which seemed to probe
the corners of her mind.

'Why don't we forget last night and start again?'
he suggested.

His hand was still on her shoulder, but the pressure of his fingers had slackened. She was conscious of his towering height and the ease with which, if he chose, he could swing her up in his arms. She had never been more aware of herself as a female than she was with this tall, powerful man.

'Very well,' she agreed reluctantly. 'I—I don't think you'll find any changes in the grounds since you lived here. Except for the loss of the elms. I expect you know about Dutch elm disease.'

'Yes, and now other trees are being affected by something similar, I hear. Has your grandfather done anything about replacing the elms which had to be felled?'

'He had a forestry expert to advise him about it, and I think he consulted your father's solicitors before going ahead. He's been a punctilious tenant.'

'I don't doubt it,' was all Roderick said. Nothing about being sorry he had to ask them to leave sooner than they expected.

Clearly he was a man with little regard for conventional politeness, or indeed any of the conventions.

Yesterday she had been so overwhelmed by his remarkable likeness, full-face, to Colonel Piers Anstruther that she hadn't noticed the ruthless lines of his profile; the aggressive thrust of the chin below the wide sensual mouth. The aquiline nose and heavy eyelids reminded her slightly of a bird of prey.

No doubt Piers had had the same look, but it wasn't apparent in the portrait, which showed only the charm of his face when he was relaxed and amused, and nothing of the strong driving force which had made him a colonel when he was several years younger than the man beside her.

Rather surprisingly, the part of the grounds in which Roderick seemed to be most interested was the kitchen garden. It was enclosed by a high wall of old rose-red bricks supported by massive buttresses, which formed sheltered bays for fruit trees and cold frames.

One of the gardeners was working there, and Roderick had a conversation with him to which Flower listened without really paying attention. She was vaguely aware that it was about fertilisers and pesticides, but she was more interested in studying Roderick while his attention was given to the elderly gardener.

The man was an old-age pensioner who worked part-time, and who knew that his services would be welcomed by the owner of every large garden for miles around if he chose to desert the manor. He was always civil to her, but Abel considered him a surly fellow who answered in monosyllables and whose manner was far from respectful.

He wasn't sullen with Roderick, she noticed. Perhaps it was because Roderick spoke to him as an equal, not in the peremptory tone adopted by Abel when addressing his employees at the house, although not those in the works.

Or it might be that the old man had heard who was staying at the house and had a higher regard for the local landed gentry than for a jumped-up outsider.

The expression 'jumped-up' was one Flower had heard in the village shop when she had walked in on a conversation which had ended so abruptly, and in such a tangible atmosphere of embarrassment, that she would have been a fool not to guess who had been the subject of the discussion.

It seemed both sad and unfair that her grand-father, despite his lavish donations to local good causes and other efforts to win popularity, would never achieve what he sought. Whereas Roderick, after years away, could at once command the esteem and deference enjoyed by his father.

They were on their way to the orangery, now used as a greenhouse, when she heard a small child's voice and saw her two-year-old nephew Matthew scampering towards her, followed, some way behind, by his mother.

Wondering what Roderick and her brother's wife would make of each other, she said, 'Here comes my sister-in-law,' before she ran to meet Matthew and scoop him up in a hug.

They had exchanged smacking kisses, and his small arms were round her neck as she said, 'Hello, Sharon. This is Sir Roderick Anstruther, who arrived from America yesterday.'

Before her marriage Sharon Dursley had been a packer at the factory and a local beauty queen. Abel had opposed the match, wanting Stephen to do better for himself. But Flower thought Sharon was perfect for him. She was still, after four years of marriage, amazed at her luck in capturing the boss's grandson. In her eyes he could do no wrong, which helped to bolster his ego against Abel's constant criticisms.

Although now the mother of two children—she would have left the baby at home with her au pair—she had kept the curvaceous figure of her beauty-contest days, and was wearing a pale blue flying-suit with the legs tucked inside silver cowboy boots and the top unzipped to reveal a clinging pink turtleneck sweater. She was always heavily made up, with false eyelashes and—for the time being—red hair set in the latest style. In spite of her tarty appearance, she was a nice cheerful girl and an excellent cook.

'How do you do, Mrs Dursley?' said Roderick, shaking her hand with its long plum-red nails.

A little of Flower's antagonism subsided as she noted that his attitude to Sharon was neither subtly patronising nor in any way predatory.

'Pleased to meet you. Goodness, aren't you tall?' said Sharon with a nervous titter.

He said, 'Yes, it's a nuisance sometimes, as you'll find out if your son grows up to be a beanstalk. I was as tall as my father by the time I was fourteen. Finding clothes to fit me was quite a problem.'

'I shouldn't think Matt will be tall. Steve's not, is he, Flow?'

Sharon never used anyone's full name if it could be abbreviated.

Inwardly Flower winced every time her own name was shortened to rhyme with cow. But she hadn't said anything to her sister-in-law, who received enough strictures from Abel. In spite of his frequent claims to be a man of the people, it was a sharp thorn in his side that his grandson's in-laws ran a mobile fish-and-chip shop which, every other Wednesday, came to the village near the manor.

'We're just going to look at the orangery, and then we'll go back to the house and have coffee,' she explained to Sharon. Then, remembering what Roderick had said as they'd left the breakfast table, 'or perhaps we'll have milk, like Matthew.'

She set him on his feet. Like his father, he was heavier than he ought to have been, rather a lump to hold for more than a few minutes.

The child held up his arms and began to whine, which invariably made his parents give in to him.

'Be a good boy, Matt,' said Sharon, but her tone lacked the gentle authority which Flower could exert when she had her nephew to herself.

He ignored her, continuing to grizzle until he was swept off his feet and perched high on Roderick's broad shoulders. For a moment it seemed that, finding himself such a long way from earth, he might begin to howl in earnest. Then, his chubby legs firmly held and his small hands grasping his steed's dark hair, he recovered his good humour.

'I always think this place would make a super indoor swimming-pool and jacuzzi,' said Sharon as they approached the orangery, built in 1818 to house orange and lemon trees and other exotic plants.

'You're right. That's an excellent idea,' Roderick agreed with her, much to Flower's surprise. 'Are there many jacuzzis in England? They're extremely popular in America.'

'Saunas are nice too.' Encouraged by the success of her suggestion, Sharon relaxed, and began to chatter with her usual vivacity.

About an hour later when she was leaving, and Flower was seeing her to her car while Roderick was escorted round the staff's part of the house by Watson, Sharon said, 'I think he's smashing. Not a bit toffee-nosed. Is he married?'

Flower shook her head.

'Then, if I was you, I'd snaffle him before Lady Prudence and her stuck-up friends get to hear he's back.'

'They're welcome to him, Sharon. He's not my type.'

'That's like saying Richard Gere isn't your type. Some men are everyone's type. You could be the next Lady Anstruther if you put your mind to it. Then you wouldn't have to leave here. You know it's going to upset you. Your grandad won't mind, not really. But you will. You love the manor.'

'When did Dodo tell Stephen? Last night?'

'No, Steve heard about it at work this morning. He rang up to tell me to come over and have a look at him—Rod, I mean. With the old man being riled about the way Steven handled things yesterday, there wasn't much chance of him being invited to meet him. Poor old Steve: he's doing his best, but you'd never think it the way your grandad goes on at him. There are times when I think we'd be happier living in a council house, like Mum and Dad did when they was our age. Oh, I like having my own car and everything, but not if it's going to make Steve old before his time. He comes home washed out... not a bit like he used to be.'

She began to cry.

Flower put both arms round her and hugged her. 'Poor Sharon. Try not to cry. You'll worry Matthew... not to mention ruining your make-up.'

Fortunately the little boy was some distance away from them, picking up pieces of gravel.

Sharon pulled herself together. 'I'm sorry,' she mumbled, sniffing. 'But I love Steve, Flow. I really do. I know some people make snide remarks about me being a gold-digger, but I'd have fallen for Steve if he hadn't had a penny. I hate the old man for what he's doing to him. Why can't he retire and leave us in peace? I don't know how you stand living with him. Mum was only saying the other day you must have the patience of a saint.'

'He doesn't badger me as much as he does Stephen. If we do have to leave the manor perhaps I can persuade him to take me on a world cruise and give Stephen a breathing space and a chance to handle things his way,' said Flower.

After her sister-in-law had driven away she walked slowly back to the house, wondering what her grandfather's lawyers had recommended him to do.

Sharon's advice to snaffle Roderick before the daughters of various aristocratic families in the area got wind of his return reminded her that yesterday, in her bath before dinner, she had felt that her life up to date had been merely an overture and now, at last, the curtain was rising. If she hadn't consciously thought of marriage the idea had been there at the back of her mind.

Apart from what had happened later, in the morning-room, she saw now there could never be anything between them but a short-lived liaison. Marriage was out of the question.

Roderick might be less of a snob than her grandfather in many ways, but even so he would never encumber himself with her motley collection of relations. Not many men would be able to stomach Dodo, she thought gloomily. Even his own grandson couldn't.

The thought of going on a long cruise on a liner full of elderly people—for who else had the time to spare nowadays?—depressed her almost as much as the thought of vacating the manor.

Never again to see the drifts of daffodils in spring. Never again to hear the cuckoo calling from the beech woods, or to have tea on the terrace where, between the mellow old flagstones, there grew mosses and little creeping plants.

Where else, if they moved from the manor, would they have an old-fashioned Christmas with a tall tree and crackling log fires, and home-grown holly and mistletoe?

There was something about this old house she would always miss if she left it. She had known that one day she must leave it when she married. But she hadn't guessed what a painful wrench it would be to have to leave for another reason, without the compensation of being in love.

As she paused in the hall to check that some plants had been watered—a task which was sometimes neglected if she didn't keep an eye on them—John came to tell her there had been an accident.

'But Sir Roderick is dealing with it, miss. It appears he's a qualified doctor.'

'I know. What's happened, John?'

'Mrs Wood was standing on a chair in the pantry and she fell off and hit her head.'

'Poor Mrs Wood seems to be accident-prone. It's not long since she sprained her wrist and before that she scalded her leg at home.'

She found Mrs Wood, one of the corps of part-time cleaners, being attended to in what had been the housekeeper's sitting-room until the last one had left and Flower had decided to take the reins of the household into her own hands.

Roderick's shirt-sleeves were rolled back from sinewy forearms, and he was applying a thick pad of gauze to one side of the woman's forehead.

There was blood on her face and spattered on her nylon overall. She kept saying, 'Oh, dear...oh, dear,' in a faint voice.

'It looks worse than it is,' he said as Flower went to the other side of Mrs Wood and took her hand in a comforting clasp. 'Head injuries always bleed a lot. It's not a very large gash. I've applied two temporary sutures made from twists of plaster, but I think she should be seen by her own doctor. What's the set-up here now? Is Dr Kerr still going strong?'

'No, he's been retired for some years. There are three young doctors in group partnership. I'll ring up the surgery and tell them I'm bringing her in. Watson, would you have my car brought round, please? And we'll need a couple of rugs to keep Mrs Wood warm. What about a cup of tea for her?' she asked with an interrogative glance at Roderick.

'It's being made.'

Having finished fixing the pad in place, he dipped a swab of cotton-wool in warm water and began to wipe the blood from the cleaner's face.

'I'm sorry to be a nuisance, sir...miss,' she murmured anxiously.

'Don't apologise, Mrs Wood. You didn't do it on purpose. You must spend the rest of the day in bed...letting your family wait on you for a change,' said Flower, still holding her hand. 'Isn't it lucky we happened to have a doctor in the house?' She was watching the swift expert way he was dealing with the smears.

There wasn't room for Mrs Wood and Roderick in the Ferrari, and when Flower came back from the surgery she found him returning to the house from near the main gate. She stopped to pick him up.

'How long have you had this?' he asked as the red car moved forwards.

'Nearly a year. It was Dodo's surprise for my last birthday.'

'The girl with everything.'

'Is that a jibe?'

'A statement of fact. It must be difficult for your friends to find something to give you that you haven't already got.'

'My close friends don't have any problems,' she said, thinking of the presents given to her by Emily and Andrew, none of them costly but all of them chosen with love and understanding so that their Christmas and birthday presents were among her dearest possessions.

'Do you have many close friends?'

'Only two... a girl who was at school with me, and her husband.'

'It's the same for me, in reverse. My closest friend was an intern with me. He was killed in an automobile accident last year.'

'Oh... I'm sorry.' Flower spoke sincerely. She knew what a horrible void it would leave in her life if anything happened to either of the Fairchilds.

'What made it worse for his parents and his wife was that he was exceptionally gifted and would have done a lot of good, and the man who killed him— and survived—was a drunken politician, a species I don't much care about even when they're sober,' he said in a biting tone. 'He and Kim had planned to start their family this year. But at least she has an interesting job which has helped her to get through the worst months.'

Something in his tone made her wonder if, in sharing Kim's grief for his dead friend, he had come to feel more than friendship for her.

'What does she do?' she asked.

'She's a nutritionist. So was George. They both took their Master of Science degrees in biochemistry at the University of California Medical School. Then they came east and I met them.'

'I'm not sure what a nutritionist does.'

'She prescribes diets for people suffering from nutritional deficiencies. For instance, you said this morning—perhaps not seriously—that you worried about the state of your nails. If you consulted Kim she might advise you to take two or three teaspoons of powdered kelp every day.'

'What's kelp?'

'It's a type of seaweed full of minerals, notably iodine, which, among other things, can help to cure splitting nails. Although we're polluting the seas now, the ocean bed is still richer and less contaminated than the soils on land. Therefore undersea flora contains lots of chemical elements we no longer get from land-grown crops.'

'I must try it. My nails aren't as strong as I'd like them to be.'

It sounded as if he had spent a lot of time listening to Kim talking about her work, she thought.

'I prefer them to your sister-in-law's talons,' said Roderick. 'She's a very pretty girl, but she'd be even more attractive without those red claws.'

'How observant you are. Most men don't notice those details.'

'Doctors notice—or they should. Sometimes details can be important clues to a diagnosis.'

'This clinic you've spoken about—how do you plan to finance it?' she asked. 'It sounds an expensive project, and you've given me the impression that you have rather limited resources.'

'I have no resources at all, other than my qualifications and the house,' he agreed casually. 'My parents only rented the house they had in Arizona. Although they had some medical insurance, it didn't cover my mother's treatment in full. My father was in debt when he died. But one can usually find backers for a well-founded project.'

'It's possible my grandfather might put up some funds—if the clinic was housed somewhere else and you let us remain at the manor until the end of the renewal period.'

'The house is essential to the project, and I want to live here again. As I've told you, my parents rented places. Twice they had to move out of properties they liked because their lease wasn't renewable. They accepted those moves as one of the hazards of tenancy. They knew they would find somewhere else which, after a time, would suit them equally well. I'm sure you'll find the same thing.'

They were nearly back at the manor now. She dropped the subject. As they turned the last bend in the drive she saw Abel's Rolls-Royce disappearing through the archway into the stable-yard.

She dropped Roderick outside the main door and drove round to garage her car. Then she entered the house by a back way and hovered outside the downstairs cloakroom until her grandfather emerged.

It was obvious at once that he was in a good humour. Which meant he must have a strong case. Knowing Roderick had gone up to his room to tidy himself before lunch, she said, 'So you're going to fight him?'

'Fight him . . . and beat him,' he confirmed. 'But if Anstruther's got any sense it won't go to court.

Litigation's an expensive business, which I can afford but he can't. We'll settle the matter on my terms.'

Flower found she couldn't share his triumph. She didn't want to move out, yet she knew she could never be comfortable while the rightful occupant of the house was barred from it.

'I thought you'd be pleased,' said Abel, detecting that her feelings were mixed. 'I suppose now you're going to feel sorry for him. You're too soft-hearted, that's your trouble.'

'I—I wish there weren't a conflict between our interests and his.'

'Maybe there isn't,' he answered.

'What do you mean?'

'Maybe we can reach a compromise. You're not having lunch in those boots, are you? It's time you were changed. I'm hungry.'

As she ran upstairs she met and passed Roderick coming down. He had brushed his thick springy hair and changed his blue shirt for a pink one.

She had assumed that Abel would discuss the lease at the lunch table. To her surprise he said nothing about it, but talked of the government's policies and his own views on how they should handle the country's economic problems.

Flower was even more perplexed when, at the end of the meal, he said with unwonted formality, 'If you'll excuse us, my dear, we'll have our coffee in the study and join you in the lounge later.'

She was left on her own for the better part of half an hour, anxiously awaiting the outcome of their private discussion. Why her grandfather had excluded her from it, she could not imagine.

At last she heard voices in the corridor. A few
moments later the door was opened by Roderick,
and Abel marched in, looking even more pleased
with himself.

Roderick's expression was totally inscrutable. It
was impossible to guess what he was thinking.

'I've asked him to spend another night here,' her
grandfather announced, 'I told you we might reach
a compromise, and we have. Now it's up to you,
Flower.'

'Up to me?' she repeated blankly.

'I've told him I'll waive my option—on one condition,' said Abel.

'The condition being that you should remain
here ... permanently,' Roderick continued. 'Not as
the tenant's granddaughter but as the owner's wife.
Your grandfather thinks it would be a good idea
for us to get married, Flower. I admit to being surprised at first; but, now that I've thought it over,
it seems a very sound suggestion. How does it strike
you?'

CHAPTER FIVE

AFTER a long pause Flower said, 'I think you must both be out of your minds. Is this some kind of sick joke? If so, it doesn't amuse me.'

'I knew you'd flare up at first,' said her grandfather, 'but it's no joke. It's sound sense, my girl. Just you give yourself time to consider it from every angle, as I have this morning. In the first place——'

Roderick interrupted him. 'I think you should leave this to me, Mr Dursley,' he broke in firmly.

The old man was not accustomed to being interrupted, or to taking a back seat. For a moment he glowered at the younger man in a way which, had it been his grandson who had spoken out of turn, would have made Stephen mutter an apology.

Roderick was made of sterner stuff than her brother. He met her grandfather's glare with a level and unwavering look, which evidently made the old man realise that here was someone who he couldn't make kowtow to him.

'Oh . . . oh, very well, if you think so. I'll leave you alone, then.'

'Wait a minute!' Flower said angrily. 'It seems to me that I'm the one whose presence is unnecessary. You two have cooked up this scheme. I'm sure you can handle the details without reference to me. My feelings are really immaterial. I'd be interested to know how much money is involved in the deal. Don't try to pretend you haven't discussed the financial side. I shan't believe you.'

'Yes, we've talked about money,' Roderick agreed. 'Naturally your grandfather wants to ensure that you continue to enjoy the standard of living to which you've been accustomed. Clearly I haven't the means to keep you in that style, although I expect a dramatic improvement in my income when the clinic is a going concern.'

'I don't go along with this clinic,' Abel put in. 'I'd rather see the house kept up in the old style—privately. On the other hand, I take Rod's point that he has to have something to occupy him. I've offered him a chance to show what he can do in the business world, but he's turned it down flat. That being so, I'm prepared to make him a substantial interest-free loan, and to give you a generous settlement, Flower. It's all going to come to you and your brother sooner or later, so it makes no odds in the long run.'

Her eyes flashed angrily. 'I see... and my piece of the action is a title, and a husband with whom I have as little in common as Consuelo Vanderbilt and the ninth Duke of Marlborough?'

'Now there's no call to take that tone, Flower,' her grandfather said with a frown.

Roderick said equably, 'But that match foundered on the fact that he was in love with someone else and she had been bullied into the marriage by her tyrannical mother. Neither factor applies in our case. Now, if you'd leave us alone, Mr Dursley...'

This time the old man nodded and stumped out of the room.

As soon as they were on their own, Roderick said, 'Why don't we sit down?'

He indicated a sofa but, deliberately, Flower chose a chair some distance from any others.

Looking faintly amused by this manoeuvre, he settled himself in a relaxed posture on the sofa.

'My attitude to marriage has been influenced by a controversial book published by an American psychotherapist, Dr Paul Hauck,' he said. 'Have you heard of him?'

'No, and in my opinion a lot of psychologists and psychiatrists are too unbalanced themselves to advise other people how to live,' she answered curtly.

When Roderick smiled, it crinkled the lines round his eyes and formed two oddly appealing creases in his cheeks. Every time they appeared she felt the tug of his attraction, as she did when he made certain gestures with his long hands or when a laugh showed his white teeth.

'There's something in that,' he agreed. 'But if you had read Hauck's theories on marriage you'd have been as impressed as I was by the good sense of his reasoning.'

Flower gave a sceptical shrug. 'What are his theories?'

'He believes that falling in love is a romantic myth. He defines a successful marriage as one based on clear insights as to what the partners want from each other; not what they can give each other. Some people find that a shocking idea. You may be one of them.'

He had kindled an unwilling interest. She said, 'What does he mean by "what the partners want from each other"?'

Roderick eyed her for a moment. 'Perhaps you've never thought out what you need to make you happy. For one person it might be a life of travel and adventure, for another staying in the same place.'

He suddenly sprang to his feet and began to pace back and forth, his hands in his trouser pockets.

'Some people need parties, others solitude. Some can rub along without much money, others must have certain luxuries. Most very young people don't understand their own natures, which is why Hauck thinks that, ideally, marriage should be illegal for anyone under, say, twenty-five.'

He changed direction and came to stand by her chair.

'He would probably think you were too young... although experience is what counts.'

How much experience did he think she had had? Flower wondered. And by experience did he mean of life in general, or of men? She had an impulse to point out that if he meant the latter she was by no means as experienced as he seemed to suppose.

Before she could make any comment, Roderick resumed his pacing.

'Hauck's premise is that marriage is a business; a company of two run to satisfy the healthy self-interests of the partners.'

He glanced at her. 'We both want to live in this house, which gives us a strong mutual interest. Also, I've arrived at the age when I should prefer what a famous actress called the deep, deep peace of the double bed after the hurly-burly of the chaise-longue.'

It was a tacit admission that he had had a great deal of experience, she thought. Well, she didn't mind that. Single men seized their opportunities. They always had and always would, and men with

Roderick's magnetism had more opportunities than most. What she found impossible to judge was whether, having made the most of his chances while he was a bachelor, he would be capable of fidelity to his wife.

'I'd like to have children,' he went on, 'so I need to choose a girl who likes them ... as you demonstrated that you did this morning.'

'And, above all, you'd like the loan my grandfather has offered you,' she said with a sting in her voice.

'That too—yes, I don't deny it. There's important work to be done here—life-saving work. I'll take any help I can get, as you would if you felt you had a mission.'

'I wouldn't describe a luxurious clinic for rich private patients as a mission,' she retorted. 'It's another exercise in that healthy self-interest recommended by your Dr Hauck.'

'You don't agree with his theories? That's my fault for putting them over badly. When you read them in full you'll be more impressed. I'll see if I can get you a copy of his book. In the meantime try analysing your temperament, working out what you need to make you content and deciding if I can supply it.'

'I already know that you can't,' she said shortly. 'I believe in *un*selfish love.'

'So did the thousands of people who went through the divorce courts this year,' he said drily. 'The last time I saw some statistics, there were over one hundred and fifty thousand divorces a year in this country; and for every couple who broke up their marriage there were others who knew they were living with a bad mistake. Marriage is a great institution. I'm sure it will still be with us a hundred years hence. But that isn't to say that the reasons why people marry shouldn't be revised and adapted to produce a higher success rate.'

Flower said, 'What does Dr Hauck consider the wrong reasons for marriage?'

Roderick paused by the table on which stood a Chelsea figure of Apollo playing a lyre.

He picked it up to study the delicately modelled *bocage* of flowers and leaves surrounding the god before he answered, 'One of the wrong reasons is to avoid being unmarried. That can motivate both sexes, apparently; although it's women who are more likely to marry because they're afraid of independence, or because they've had sex with a man and don't want to be thought promiscuous.

'To escape an unhappy home is another common reason, and some people actually make what Hauck calls a "therapeutic" marriage, by which he means the need to feel superior to a partner who's weak and inadequate. It explains why women stick with a man who drinks or gambles.'

He replaced the porcelain figure on the table. 'You must have met people who fit those categories,' he said with a glance over his shoulder.

'Yes, I have. But those aren't arguments against love. They're merely examples of its absence.'

'On the contrary, most of the couples who marry for reasons of that sort are under the impression that they are in love. Hauck lists four rational motives for marriage.'

Tapping his right forefinger against the fingers of his left hand, he listed them. 'Companionship... convenient sex... children... a desirable life-style. When they outweigh the neurotic reasons, the marriage or partnership has a good chance. Incidentally, he defines companionship as liking to have someone around for reasons other than sex or the kind of services you can pay to have done for you, such as cooking or household odd jobs.'

She said, 'You can't seriously put forward companionship as a reason for me to marry you. We only met yesterday afternoon.'

'And I'm not suggesting we should marry tomorrow afternoon. There's a lot to be done before we arrive at that point. It may have to wait for some months. We'll have plenty of time to make friends. But one thing we have established is that we find each other sexually exciting.' He began strolling towards her. 'Haven't we?'

When Flower didn't answer he suddenly quickened his pace to a swift stride. She saw his intention in his eyes and sprang up to try to evade him. But he sidestepped to intercept her. The next moment she was held fast in his arms.

'Please let me go,' she said coldly.

'Haven't we?' Roderick repeated.

How could she deny it when the feel of his arms and the contact with his tall strong body made her instantly weak at the knees?

But she wasn't going to tell him that.

'Do you make a habit of forcing your attentions on women?'

He looked down at her, laughter in his eyes. 'Most women like a little gentle coercion.'

'Is that something else you learned from the great Dr Hauck?'

'No, from observation and experience.'

'Of which, I'm sure, you have an extremely wide range. But there are exceptions to every rule, and I *don't* like brute strength being used on me. So now will you please let me go?'

His response was to bend his head and press a firm kiss on her lips. She had no chance to jerk her face aside because his hand was at the back of her head, holding it still while his mouth moved slowly on hers.

There was nothing brutal about it. That she could have withstood more effectively.

But to maintain passive resistance while being kissed with great tenderness by a man who not only had every natural advantage but was also an imaginative lover—that was next to impossible.

Against her will, she found herself yielding and responding.

Presently he murmured against her cheek, 'I've wanted you from the moment you walked in here yesterday...and you felt the same way. Admit it.'

'No...no...'

Her denial was stifled by another long sensuous kiss.

Sometimes, in other men's arms, she had felt the first stirrings of pleasure. But never this strange loss of will, this heart-racing, pulsing excitement as his hands moved over her back, pressing her closer to him.

Somehow, of their own volition, her arms had crept round his neck and her fingers were in his thick hair.

What happened then was very odd. Suddenly it seemed to her that they were no longer almost strangers, but passionate lovers, saying farewell... Piers and a girl of his time, locked in their final embrace.

The feeling was so compelling, so real, that she found herself clinging to him and kissing him with a wildness she hadn't known was in her.

Her breasts and thighs quivered and throbbed. The evidence of his desire which had put her to flight the night before was no longer alarming. She wanted him to possess her... as he had before, many times. They belonged to each other... heart and mind... body and soul.

It was he who broke off the embrace, suddenly pushing her from him with a smothered exclamation.

Dazed and completely disoriented, she gazed in bewilderment as he turned his back and moved away.

Piers... my love...

Perhaps she didn't say the words aloud but only in her mind. He didn't react. An instant later she knew he wasn't Piers. It had been an illusion, a waking dream, yet vivid enough to leave her aching with longing, her whole body shaking as she sucked in air like an exhausted runner.

After a moment or two she sank back into the chair from which she had sprung when she'd seen that Roderick intended to kiss her. She felt even more shaken than she had the night before. Coming on top of his amazing, cold-blooded proposal, the storm of emotion which had just ranged through her like a tornado was too much to take.

She closed her eyes, striving for composure, trying to come to terms with the fact that what she had refused to admit to him was true. She had wanted him on sight—but only because he was the incarnation of her daydreams.

'Flower.'

She opened her eyes to find him standing beside her, holding two glasses, one of which he was offering to her.

'What is it?'

'A little of your grandfather's excellent brandy.'

On the point of saying she never touched it, she changed her mind.

'You won't deny now that there's a special chemistry between us,' he said drily.

She sipped a little of the spirit. It was Remy Martin's Fine Champagne VSOP, her grandfather's favourite brand. Although a philistine in many ways, he did appreciate fine wines and spirits.

At length she said, 'That doesn't mean I accept that we could have a successful marriage.'

'Unsatisfactory sex is the rock on which a lot of unsuccessful marriages have foundered,' was Roderick's matter-of-fact reply.

'I've never heard of a good one based on sex and nothing else.'

'Ours won't be based on that alone.'

He didn't say 'wouldn't be', she noticed. He took it for granted that he could bend her to his will.

'Perhaps that demonstration of our physical rapport has made you forget the three other good reasons for marriage. Children . . . companionship . . . and a mutually desirable way of life,' he reminded her.

'What about my grandfather?' she asked. 'Where does he fit into this plan? Is he to continue to live here? I'm certain that wouldn't work on a permanent basis. You'd be at loggerheads within a month.'

'Undoubtedly.'

Later she was to remember the satanic gleam of amusement which accompanied the dry comment.

'However, I don't think he'll mind finding somewhere else to live, provided that you remain here and your children grow up here,' Roderick went on. 'Shall we call him in and put that point to him?'

'If you wish—as long as you realise that I'm not committing myself to anything,' she added hurriedly.

'Naturally not,' he agreed smoothly. But his eyes were mocking. He was sure she would agree eventually.

She watched him walk out of the room with the long graceful stride so different from her grandfather's self-important strut or Stephen's slouching gait.

Roderick moved with the long-jointed elegance of a thoroughbred horse, his back upright, his shoulders held back. Probably, as a small boy, he had had a nanny to inculcate the habits which now were second nature to him.

No one had told Stephen or Flower not to slump. It was only when she had been transferred to her boarding-school that her faulty posture had been noticed and gradually corrected by remedial exercises and frequent reminders from the mistresses to sit up straight and not drag her feet.

Thinking about Roderick's patrician bearing made her realise that all her previous relationships with men had ended because, sooner or later, their habits had become as irksome to her as her poor posture had been to the mistresses at school.

So far, nothing about Roderick's appearance or behaviour jarred on her. But how, on the strength of less than twenty-four hours' acquaintance, could either of them be sure that they were really compatible?

She felt that she had known him forever, but she knew that that was an illusion because for more than twelve years she had indulged in romantic fantasies about a man who looked like him. The real Roderick Anstruther was a stranger, a fact she must not allow herself to forget.

The two men came back into the room. Her grandfather gave her a sharp look, but he didn't say anything.

It was Roderick who said, 'Flower can't be expected to make up her mind immediately. She needs time to think things over. But if, as I hope, she decides to do me the honour of becoming my wife it will mean that most of the house will be given over to the clinic, with the private quarters reduced to a minimum. There will only be room for the two of us and, in due course, our children. I think you have already taken that into account. But she feels you might not have done so.'

There was a fractional pause in which it was clear that Abel had not considered this aspect of the matter.

He did not take long to react. 'So you don't want me living with you, eh?' he said, flicking beady glances at each of them in turn.

Without hesitation, Roderick answered, 'You know as well as I do, sir, that there can be only one master in a house. For us both to live here would be an impossibility... and, when we disagreed, divided loyalties would put an intolerable strain on Flower.'

'I suppose you're right,' the old man said grudgingly.

It was, as far as she could remember, the first time he had ever agreed with a point of view he had not put forward himself.

'Yes, you are right,' he added, in a more positive tone. 'Well, that's not a problem. I'll find somewhere else to live.'

Whereupon, being without his cellphone, he flung his considerable weight into a chair, which creaked under the strain, and made a call to his secretary. Without any preliminary, he said, 'Get on to those estate agents who found the manor for me and tell them I want details of all the freehold houses for sale within a thirty-mile radius of this place. Freehold, mind.' He banged the receiver back on the rest.

Flower often wondered if the day would come when his secretary would tire of seldom being addressed by name and even more rarely receiving the everyday courtesies. But her grandfather paid well, and presumably his secretary found her salary adequate compensation for his rudeness.

'You certainly believe in "action this day",' was Roderick's comment.

Abel nodded. 'I learnt that from Sir Winston Churchill. Once he'd made up his mind he wouldn't stand for delays. I'm the same. I'll be out of this house in under a month...you can take my word on that.'

'Now hold on, Dodo...I haven't agreed to marry Roderick yet,' said Flower. 'It's absurd for you to rush out and buy somewhere else when nothing is settled between us.' Her chin lifting, her eyes sparkling defiance, she looked from one man to the other. 'I warn you...if either of you tries to coerce me...I'll dig my heels in. I'm not as malleable as I was when you stamped on my career plans, Dodo. If need be, I could support myself now. I have some qualifications...and I also have some investments.'

Seeing her grandfather's surprise, she went on, 'I don't spend as much on clothes as you seem to think. Some of my quarterly allowance goes into a contingency fund. The flat is in my name and I have enough money behind me to pay the overheads for at least a year.'

'Well, I'll be bu—blowed!' exclaimed Abel, who normally moderated his language only in the presence of parsons, whom he held in respect except when they had trendy tendencies. 'I thought all you knew about money was how to spend it. Investments, eh? Who's been advising you?'

'No one. I've used my own judgement. I've heard you say dozens of times that if financial advisers really knew what they were doing they wouldn't be managing other people's money, they'd be multimillionaires themselves.'

'It sounds as if your granddaughter has inherited some of your financial acumen, Mr Dursley,' said Roderick. 'Perhaps, instead of discouraging her ambitions, you should have let her have her head.'

'If she'd come to me with a sensible idea I might have done,' said Abel. 'But she wanted to go to art school and I weren't having that. They're a loose-living lot, art students. I didn't send her to a posh school and have her made into a lady for her to go mixing with punks and smoking pot and worse.'

'I tried smoking pot at school, Dodo,' Flower informed him. 'It was smuggled in by a girl whose father was a peer and who is now a heroin addict, poor thing. But she didn't influence me to go the same way. I was a lot more likely to make a mess of my life by having nothing to do than by studying design and wearing way-out clothes for a year or two.'

'If I'd known there was someone leading you into bad ways I'd have had her thrown out,' he said angrily. 'You're not smoking that stuff now, are you?'

Flower made a negative gesture. 'I only mentioned it to point out that both Emily and I were exposed to as many bad influences in the supposedly protected environment of school as we were likely to meet after school. If, at fifteen or sixteen, all your peers claim to have had sex you're a lot more likely to follow their example than you are a few years later, by which time you've realised that quite a few of them were lying just to be "in the swim".'

Any reference to sex always embarrassed her grandfather. In his youth the subject had been taboo in mixed company, and, although she knew that in a group of men with no women within earshot he would guffaw as loudly as the rest at a dirty joke, he also had a curiously prudish streak.

When the gossip columnists had implied that she was sleeping around he had shirked talking to her about her allegedly wild ways. It was not thanks to Abel's loving concern and wise counsel that she had avoided the pitfalls of promiscuity.

Perhaps sensing that the conversation had taken a tack which was not to his host's liking, Roderick said, 'I should like to go for a walk...and take Flower with me. We have a lot to learn about each other.'

Abel approved of this suggestion with a hearty, 'Good idea!'

Flower would have preferred some time alone. At the same time there were questions she wanted to ask Roderick. So she agreed to his suggestion that they go for a tramp in the countryside he had known as a boy.

The ground being dry underfoot now, they both changed into trainers before setting out.

'Why don't you have any dogs? Don't you like animals?' he asked as they left the house.

'I do, but my grandfather doesn't. He was bitten by a dog as a child and it put him off them. Did you have dogs when you lived here?'

'Always. My father had three gun dogs, old-fashioned curly-coated labradors. Mother had a black pug and a white whippet, and I had a very intelligent black and tan mongrel.'

'What happened to them when your parents went to America?'

'The labradors were given to a gamekeeper and my mother took her dogs with her. My dog Tom got run over. As he was quite badly injured the person who was in charge of him while I was at school—this was after my parents had moved to Arizona—had him put down. It was probably the right decision but I was rather upset by it.'

For a moment, seeing his expression, Flower felt a pang of pity for the boy who, having lost his home and with his parents far away, had heard the news that his dog was dead. Privileged he might have been, but not immune from pain.

But, just as she was thinking that, in that respect if no other, they had something in common, he turned to look at her.

'What sort of dog would you like to have when we're married?' His eyes held a glint of teasing.

'You talk as if it were *fait accompli. It's not!*' she retorted emphatically. 'Frankly, I don't care for that remark you made to Dodo about there only being room for one master in a household. If you've got the idea that, because I've allowed my grandfather to dominate my life to date, you can easily dominate the rest of it, think again. I shall never marry except on an equal-partnership basis. If you can't accept that, forget the whole idea.'

'I accept it unreservedly,' he answered. 'Husbands and wives should always be equal partners. What puzzles me is why you allowed your grandfather to talk you out of the career you wanted.'

'He didn't talk me out of it.' She explained briefly what had happened. 'At that time I was too young to see that disowning me was a bluff. He loves me as much as I love him. If he threatens to cut me off if I won't agree to marry you, I'll do what I should have then . . . call his bluff.'

'Perhaps instinct told you life had something else lined up . . . that you weren't cut out for a career. Not all women are. Some have gifts which are best expressed in making a home and helping their husband and children to fulfil their ambitions,' he said. 'It's a perfectly honourable role . . . and far more worthwhile than many of the jobs your sex does outside the home. The only thing wrong with being a housewife is that too few women who are feel a sense of accomplishment. They admit to it rather than proclaim it.'

She stopped short and turned to face him. 'But you yourself raised an eyebrow when you found out I ran the manor instead of working in London.'

Roderick checked his stride to look down at her. 'Only because of your age. I don't believe women should be brainwashed into working outside the home unless they want to or circumstances oblige it. But I do think that every woman should have some experience of the rat race so that she knows the pressures and problems her children are going to have to grapple with.'

He paused before adding. 'It would have done you good to have gone to art school and tried your luck in the job market. But, if you had, you wouldn't have been so well qualified to help me adapt the house to its new function ... to keep it alive and well in the twenty-first century.'

Flower began walking again. 'What exactly is its new function? You haven't explained that fully.'

'The money-making side of the operation will be a healthy heart clinic for senior executives or anyone else at risk... your grandfather, for example. I don't want to worry you, but what he eats and the way he lives are almost guaranteed to cause trouble before he's much older. And it sounds as if your brother could have problems in a few years' time.'

'I'm sure he will... I'm very worried about Stephen,' she admitted. 'His wife's worried too. This morning, before she left here, Sharon burst into tears. Their life is being made a misery because Stephen can't stand up to Dodo.'

She had not meant to confide in Roderick, but now that he had touched on the other worry lurking behind her personal dilemma she had been unable to stop herself.

He said, 'That problem may be resolved by your grandfather's being obliged to step down and hand over to Stephen. I would guess that Mr Dursley has seriously high blood-pressure. Maybe he knows it but is disregarding his doctor's advice. Maybe he doesn't know it. Hypertension is a condition some people manage to live with for quite a long time before something happens which can't be ignored. Have you discussed his health with him?'

She shook her head. 'Not really. I've tried to persuade him to have an annual check-up but he won't listen. Perhaps you can convince him it would be a sensible thing to do.'

'Doesn't he have a doctor of his own?'

'He's never needed one. I've never known him to be ill.'

'Isn't there a doctor at the works? Most large firms have some medical back-up.'

'There are excellent medical facilities for the lower-paid workers, and health insurance schemes for the senior staff. But Dodo, who could afford to go to the top consultants, won't go near a doctor. As for Stephen's GP, his advice was to take some tranquillisers. I was furious. They're the last thing my brother needs,' she said, frowning.

'In that case I'll try having a tactful word with your grandfather,' said Roderick.

For the second time Flower halted. 'I would be grateful if you would.'

At that moment her concern for her grandfather and brother was the only thought in her mind.

She was unprepared for Roderick to put his hands on her shoulders and say, with a smile, 'Is my intervention worth a kiss?'

CHAPTER SIX

WITHOUT waiting for Flower's reply, Roderick bent to kiss her lightly on the cheek. Then he turned his head, offering his cheek for her kiss.

This approach was so different from his forceful embrace in the house a little while earlier that it took her by surprise. After a moment's hesitation she put her lips to the taut brown skin presented to her.

Roderick straightened, still holding her shoulders but not with the punitive grip which had brought her to a standstill that morning.

He said, 'I want to know where I stand before I go back to the States. So you have just under a fortnight to make up your mind.'

'And if I decide to decline your proposal? What then?'

'Then I'm afraid you and your grandfather will have to find somewhere else to live and I shall have to go to the City for my financial backing, which was my intention in the first place.'

Flower drew back and he did not restrain her.

'I'm not sure that I want to stay here if the whole place is going to be changed ... filled with fat-cat businessmen. What I know of their world doesn't appeal to me. I love the manor as it is.'

'I loved it as it was,' he said drily. 'Your grandfather has been a conscientious tenant, but frankly I don't much care for the personal touches he's introduced, particularly in the library.'

She did not admit that she didn't like them herself. Instead she said, 'Are you warning me that if I marry you I shan't be allowed to arrange the house to my liking?'

'I hope we shall be like my parents and discuss any changes we want to make. Your grandfather tells me that when he first came here your parents moved in with him. It must have been pretty traumatic, losing them both when you were only ten.'

'Yes, it was a shock,' she agreed. 'But, in a way, a relief. You see, they didn't get on. They had terrible rows and that worried Stephen and me...made us feel somehow to blame. I didn't find out what it was like to be part of a happy, loving family until I went to stay with Emily Fairchild, my best friend at boarding-school. It was the first time I'd seen married people smiling at each other and laughing together the way her parents did . . . as they still do.'

No sooner had she told him this than she wondered what had possessed her to confide thoughts she had never shared with anyone but Emily.

To her astonishment he touched her cheek gently with his knuckles. 'Poor little rich girl.'

Was he mocking her? Yet there was a note in his voice which brought a curious lump to her throat. She had to turn on her heel and walk briskly on or he would have seen tears in her eyes.

'At least I've been miserable in comfort,' she said, trying to sound flippant. She didn't want him to guess how vulnerable she was. He had only to show her a little tenderness and she was lost, no defences left. 'Were your parents able to live in reasonable comfort in America?' she asked.

'They weren't people who needed much money,' he answered. 'My father took up painting. After my mother's health forced her to give up gardening she took to needlework. But I suspect she always missed the gardens here. If it hadn't been for her medical expenses they would have been comfortably off in Arizona.'

Momentarily forgetting that his father would not have inherited the manor if his brother hadn't been killed in the war, she asked, 'Were your parents only children, or do you have other relations?'

'My father's elder brother died of wounds in Italy in 1944, but my mother had three younger sisters, so I have three middle-aged aunts.'

'If I were to agree to marry you, what would they think about it?'

'Having met you, they'd think me a very lucky guy,' he said smoothly.

'I doubt that. They'd be horrified that you weren't marrying someone of your own kind.'

'In the States there are only two kinds of people... rich and poor, and it's possible for the poor to become rich if they have intelligence and drive. When your grandfather was a boy it was hard to do that in England but he succeeded. I don't aspire to make his kind of money, but by the time I hit forty I expect to have repaid all the loans and to be able to keep you in comfort if never in luxury.'

'That's sidestepping the issue. Your aunts and their husbands aren't going to approve of your marrying me.'

'I don't give a damn whether they approve or not, and you shouldn't either. You don't know my aunts and you may not like them when you meet them. The only people whose opinions matter are the people one cares about and even they don't always know best. I'm the only judge of the right girl for me to marry, and the same goes for you. Outsiders' opinions are totally unimportant.'

'You can hardly classify your aunts as outsiders...unless you have nothing to do with them. With three aunts you must have quite a few cousins.'

'Eleven cousins, but I don't have much contact with them. I've been to some of their weddings and godfathered a few of their children. When am I going to meet your brother?'

'I'll ask him and Sharon to have dinner with us tonight.'

She wanted to find out what her brother thought of Roderick. Although she and Stephen were not much alike, either in looks or temperament, sharing a childhood blighted by their parents' rows had forged a strong bond of affection between them. There were many things about Stephen which irritated her, but she loved him in spite of them and knew that he loved her and was shrewd enough to see through Roderick if her own vision of him was distorted by the strength of the physical attraction he exerted on her.

There was no chance to ask Stephen discreetly what he thought of Roderick before he and Sharon went home that night.

But when, soon after their departure, Flower went to bed she allowed enough time for them to drive back to their house, and then dialled her brother's number.

It was her sister-in-law who answered the telephone.

'It's Flower. May I speak to Stephen, please?'

'He's still in the garage. I'll call him.'

After a short pause Stephen's voice said, 'What's up?'

'I just wanted to know what you thought of Roderick?'

'Seemed OK to me.'

'Oh, *Stephen* . . . that's not an answer. I want a considered opinion . . . a potted reading of his character. How far would you trust him?'

'I don't know. I haven't thought about it. Why d'you want to know? Do you fancy him?'

After a slight hesitation, she said candidly, 'Yes, I do.'

'Well, it seems to be mutual—at least, Sharon thinks he fancies you. So where's the problem?'

'He hasn't any money. I'm what the tabloids call an heiress. Maybe that's what attracts him.'

'Maybe . . . but that's a chance you'll always have to take with guys . . . the same way I took a chance with Shar. The old man seems to like him, and he's always been paranoid about fortune-hunters.'

She had already decided not to tell Stephen about the scheme her grandfather and Roderick had cooked up between them. If she told her brother he would be bound to tell Sharon and she would tell her mother and then it would be all over the neighbourhood.

'Anyway, it's early days to be worrying about that aspect, isn't it?' said Stephen. 'You've only just met him. Time enough to worry about whether he's after your money when you've been to bed with him. When you've had him you may go off him.'

'I don't jump into bed as freely as you used to when you were single. I have other priorities,' said Flower. 'Night, Stephen.'

A few minutes later she used the house telephone to call her grandfather's room, although he might still be downstairs, talking to Roderick.

'Yes?' For some reason the telephone always emphasised the latent aggression in the old man's voice.

'There's something I want to talk about, Dodo. May I come now?'

Abel was already in bed when she entered his room. He must have come up very soon after she had.

'Have you seen the sense of it?' he asked expectantly.

Flower shook her head. 'It's not possible to make a snap decision on something as important as marriage. I came to ask you not to tell Stephen about it. He has no secrets from Sharon and she has none from her parents. If I do decide to fall in with this crazy scheme I don't want everyone knowing it's a marriage of convenience.'

'You're right: it's better kept quiet. I shan't say nowt.' Often, when they were alone, her grandfather reverted to the speech of his youth.

'The only person I shall tell is Emily,' she continued. 'If it's convenient for her I'll drive up there tomorrow morning and spend a few days with her.'

'What, and leave Rod here on his tod?' Abel also often used rhyming slang and Flower had learnt long ago that 'tod' was a reference to Tod Sloan, a jockey, Sloan rhyming with alone.

'He has things to do in London. I shall see the whole situation in sharper perspective from a distance.'

'I don't know why you don't say yes to him straight off. The more I think about it, the better the idea strikes me. He's the way I was at his age... he's got guts and the cheek of the devil. He hasn't a penny to his name, but he's not afraid to tell me to my face that there wouldn't be room for the two of us under one roof.'

'I'm surprised that didn't annoy you. You were furious when Sharon wanted a place of her own.'

'Only because your brother hid behind her skirts. I wouldn't have minded if he'd said straight out from the start they didn't want to live here with us. But he didn't have the gumption.'

'He knew what a fuss you'd make... and you did,' she reminded him. 'You roared and raged like a wounded dinosaur. Stephen can't cope with your tempers. It's not surprising. He had a lot of the stuffing knocked out of him by Dad when he was little. Dad would have liked to swipe Mum when she yelled at him, but he couldn't do that so he worked off his temper on Stephen. Luckily Stephen doesn't seem to have inherited your and Dad's temper. He never gets angry and he never lays a finger on Matthew.'

'He spoils him... they both do,' said Abel. 'They'll have trouble with that kid later, mark my words.'

'Look who's talking! You're always giving him sweets and expensive presents. He already has more toys than they've got at the crêche at the works. Don't buy him any more, Dodo. Spend the money on children who haven't got anything. The price of that life-sized stuffed baby panda you bought him last month would have paid for a Third World child to learn to read and write.'

She knew, as she spoke, that she was wasting her breath. Her grandfather only gave money to causes which might indirectly benefit him.

His room was not far from the top of the manor's main staircase. After she had said goodnight to him, as she was crossing the landing she saw Roderick coming up from the ground floor.

'I thought you would be asleep by now,' he said.

She was still in the dress she had worn for dinner and was glad that she wasn't wearing nightclothes. Last night's encounter was still vivid in her mind. As he reached the top of the flight she remembered the warmth of his hand through the flimsy top of her nightdress as his palm had curved round her breast. Almost twenty-four hours later the memory of that caress made her heartbeat quicken.

'I've been talking to Dodo.'

'About me?' he enquired.

'About Matthew, my nephew. By the way, tomorrow I'm going away for a few days.'

'When do you expect to return?'

'I can't say definitely, but probably not before Monday.'

'I see. Then I'd better give you something to remember me by.'

Before she had grasped his intention she was in his arms and he was kissing her; not lightly as he had on their walk, but in the masterful manner he had demonstrated last night and again after lunch.

Flower wanted to resist but couldn't. The fact was that each time he kissed her the more difficult she found it not to lose control completely. Being pressed to his tall muscular frame was insidiously, dangerously arousing. She felt his body responding to the close contact with hers, and her body answered the signal from his.

As the kiss grew more and more passionate she knew there was only one natural and satisfying end to this embrace. He wanted her and she wanted him and there seemed no good reason why so powerful an urge should not find fulfilment.

'Your room or mine?' Roderick murmured thickly, his lips against her mouth.

He would never know how hard it was for her to press against his chest with the heels of her hands. 'Your room for you ... mine for me.'

His hands were splayed over her hips. He pulled them more tightly against his. 'But you don't want to sleep alone and nor do I. I want to make love to you.'

'Two days ago you didn't know me. Goodnight, Roderick.' Making a determined effort to free herself, she escaped from his arms and bolted in the direction of her room.

For the second night in succession she had very little sleep, and went down to breakfast hoping it didn't show.

She had packed a small case and arranged for her car to be brought round and the case put in it.

The men were already at the table, and her grandfather was on the telephone. Roderick rose as she entered the room, and walked round to pull out her chair.

'Good morning. Sleep well?' he enquired.

'Yes, thank you,' she lied.

'I didn't. You kept me awake half the night,' he murmured while Abel was reading the riot act to whoever was on the line.

'Too bad. You shouldn't have started something
you ought to have known you couldn't finish,' she
murmured in reply.

'Heartless girl! One day soon I'll remind you of
that and punish you,' he said in an undertone.

Then Abel banged down the receiver and put an
end to the exchange.

They said goodbye in his presence. Flower made
sure of that, confident that Roderick wouldn't kiss
her with the old man standing by.

But when she offered him her hand, he lifted it
to his lips with an easy gallantry which made her
heart bounce about like a light aircraft flying
through the updraught from a busy motorway.

'Drive carefully,' he said, holding the car door
while she slid behind the wheel, trying not to give
a leg-show which would light that unnerving gleam
of desire in his eyes.

In the Ferrari, on the motorway for all but the
final ten miles, the journey north to the shires—
the heart of England's fox-hunting country—didn't
take long.

Flower drove with Kiri te Kanawa singing
Gershwin on the tape-deck. But, although the New
Zealand opera star was one of her favourite singers,
this time the exquisite voice was merely background music as she did as Roderick had advised
and tried to analyse her temperament and decide
where her deepest needs lay.

By the time she left the motorway and was following the familiar route through 'the country of
spires and squires', with its limestone cottages and
churches and weathered greenish-brown roofs clad
with the thin layers of stone known as Collyweston

slates, she was still as far from a conclusion as she had been when she'd set out.

Because what she needed above everything was to be loved. And love wasn't part of the package Roderick was offering her. It included everything else she wanted: the beautiful house she had grown to regard as 'home', a way of life which matched her natural inclinations, an attractive exciting husband, ideal conditions in which to have a large family and, least important but not to be dismissed, an entrée into the world to which Emily belonged by birth.

But did all those advantages outweigh the absence of love?

She arrived at her destination at a quarter to one. Before she had switched off the engine, her friends were hurrying out of the cottage to greet her.

'Flower... how lovely to see you. Looking stunning, as usual.' Emily hugged her and kissed her on both cheeks.

Now seven months pregnant, she was wearing a French fisherman's slop of brick-pink denim over navy blue needlecord jeans. Her mouse-brown hair was brushed smoothly back under an Alice band, and her perfect skin—lightly freckled over the bridge of her small nose—had a glow which owed nothing to make-up. She wore only a touch of pink lipstick.

'Stunning, but too thin,' said Andrew as his wife and her friend drew apart. 'Hello, Flower... good to see you.' He also kissed her on both cheeks.

Not much taller than the two tall girls, he seemed short by comparison with Roderick. His hair was fair, his eyes grey. He looked what he was: a countryman who spent almost all his waking hours in the open air, many of them on a tractor.

While Andrew took charge of Flower's case, Emily led her into the cottage, one of several lodge cottages at the entrances to the large estate owned by Andrew's father.

At one time the cottage would have been occupied by the gatekeeper and his family, but nowadays only one entrance was in regular use and, until they needed more space, South Lodge with its pointed Gothic windows and trellised porch was a convenient home for the young couple.

'Where's my goddaughter?' asked Flower, entering the sitting-room to find Jess, the grey-muzzled mother of Andrew's gun dogs, lying on the hearth rug with Emily's elderly tabby curled on a chair, but no sign of their daughter.

'She's spending the day with Griselda's mob,' Emily explained.

Griselda was her husband's elder sister whose large family ranged in age from fourteen to four.

'I thought it would be nice to have the afternoon to ourselves. Lucy is the light of my life, but she's never still for a minute, which makes it slightly hard to have a serious conversation while she's around. Perhaps I'm wrong, but I had the impression when you telephoned that you had something on your mind. Or, more probably, someone.'

'Clever of you to guess. I have.'

'Then as soon as we've got rid of Andrew we can settle down and be cosy and you can Tell All,' said Emily, stooping to take a log from the basket beside the hearth and add it to those already burning cheerfully.

They were joined by her husband. 'What would you like to drink, Flower?' he asked, going to the drinks tray. 'Sherry, or something with more kick?'

'Sherry would be lovely.' Flower glanced round the pretty room to see what new delights Emily had acquired since her last visit.

From the age of ten her friend had been a compulsive collector. Many of the things she had bought as a schoolgirl for pennies were now worth a lot of money. But it was their beauty or rarity, not their material value, that mattered to her. She had a flair not only for recognising treasures in unlikely places, but for arranging them attractively.

Every wall of the cottage was covered with paintings. There were even pictures attached to some of the doors. Every windowsill and table-top was crowded with things which had caught Emily's acquisitive eye. But somehow the overall effect, while cluttered, was totally charming—or so Flower thought. She adored her visits to South Lodge and had done her best to create a similar atmosphere at her flat in London.

Lunch consisted of a delicious soup followed by a beansprout omelette with brown bread and cheese and old-fashioned russet apples to finish. After Andrew had gone back to work, the two girls did the washing-up before settling down by the fire for an uninterrupted chat-session.

'So what would be your reaction?' Flower asked when she had described the events of the past forty-eight hours.

Emily pondered the question in silence. She was comfortably ensconced on the sofa with her shoes off and her feet up. On a small table beside her was a basket containing paper-lined hexagons of cotton to be joined together as a cot-cover for the new baby. But, although when they had first sat down she had threaded a needle with the intention of sewing while her friend confided in her, very soon she had stopped the fine stitching to concentrate on Flower's story.

'Without actually meeting Roderick Anstruther it's very hard to decide,' she said at last. 'Pity you couldn't have brought him with you and got Andrew's reaction. He's a very good judge of character...much better than I am. Did Stephen meet him? What did he make of him?'

Flower recounted her brother's advice.

'He could be right,' said Emily. 'Why didn't you let him make love to you? Were you worried that someone of his age who has never been married might have a promiscuous past?'

'Not really. I'm sure he respects his body too much to take any stupid chances with it. Obviously there have been women in his life, but I doubt if they were casual relationships. I suppose the reason I fended him off last night was because I don't want him to think I'm casual about sex. He did mention that he'd heard things about me, and you know what gossip is like...hardly ever kind or complimentary.'

'That's true,' Emily agreed. 'Why didn't you ask him straight out what he'd heard and who said it?'

'I should have done, but he...he throws me off balance.'

'No one's ever done that before, and you have known a lot of men. You're not like I was with Andrew...totally clueless about them.'

'My vast store of worldly wisdom doesn't seem to be much help in this situation,' said Flower. 'Oh,

Emily, I do envy you...having Andrew and Lucy
and very soon the new baby. You have everything
I want in life, but can I achieve it with Roderick?
It's such a step in the dark...such a risk.'

They were still discussing the matter when
Andrew came in for tea, having collected his small
daughter from his sister's house in a nearby village.

Staying with the Fairchilds reinforced Flower's
conviction that theirs was the kind of life she wanted
for herself. But talking it over with Emily, and also
taking Andrew into her confidence, didn't seem to
bring her any nearer to a decision.

On her last evening with them Andrew had to
attend a local committee meeting and, for the ump-
teenth time, his wife and his guest weighed the pros
and cons of Roderick's proposal.

'If you look at it rationally, the pluses definitely
outweigh the minuses,' said Emily. 'If you turn him
down you could wait for years for someone else to
turn up. Lovely men aren't thick on the ground.
Also you'll have to uproot yourself from the manor.
But what I see as the key point is that for the rest
of your life—especially if Mr Right never materi-
alises—you'll have to live with the thought that it
might have turned out brilliantly.'

When Flower made no comment, she went on,
'Really, the questions you have to ask yourself are:
can I make him love me? Can I make him so happy,
so comfortable that he won't want to look at anyone
else?'

They were questions which kept Flower awake
long after her hosts were asleep in their large
Victorian brass bed while she lay in one of the twin
beds in Emily's small but comfortable guest room.

And the next day, all the way home, the questions continued to nag her while, on tape, Pavarotti's thrilling lyric tenor made her long to know she *was* loved, not to be asking herself if she could *make* Roderick love her.

Before leaving South Lodge she had telephoned Watson to tell him she expected to be home for lunch.

The footman was waiting on the gravel sweep in front of the front door when she brought the car to a halt. She remembered coming back from London—could it really be less than a week ago?—and finding a hired car there, but never dreaming that its driver would turn her world upside-down.

'Hello, John. Everyone all right? No problems while I was away?'

'Everyone's fine, miss. Did you have a good trip?'

'Very nice, thank you.'

She went into the house and used the downstairs cloakroom to wash her hands before lunch, which was due to be served in ten minutes' time.

Watson was crossing the hall when she came out. 'Good afternoon, Miss Dursley. You'll find Sir Roderick and Mr Dursley in the library.'

'Sir Roderick? What is he doing here? I thought he was in London.'

'He arrived back an hour ago.'

'I see.'

But she didn't. She had not expected to see Roderick again until she had made up her mind. At the moment her decision still hung in the balance.

The library had double doors of solid mahogany, and it wasn't until Watson opened one of

them for her and stood aside that she heard
Roderick's deep, pleasant voice. As soon as he
heard the door opening, he broke off what he was
saying and rose to his feet.

The sight of him sent a surge of pleasure through
her. In that instant her mind was made up.
Whatever the risk and whatever the outcome, this
was a chance she had to take.

'Hello, Dodo.' She kissed her grandfather before
turning to Roderick and saying, with raised eyebrows, 'I didn't expect to find you here.'

He acknowledged her greeting with a slight inclination of the head. 'I hope it's a pleasant
surprise.'

Flower let the remark pass and turned to Watson,
who was hovering in the background. 'A Campari
and soda for me, please.'

'I'm glad you're back, safe and sound. I worry
about you...haring round the country in that
damned dangerous sports car,' said Abel.

'It's drivers who are dangerous, not cars,' she
said lightly. 'You know I'm a careful driver,
darling.'

'So you may be, but men don't like to be over-
taken by a pretty young blonde in a fast car. I've
driven with you. I've seen them trying to pass
you...playing the fool...showing off...breaking
the speed limit. One of these days——'

'There wasn't anyone like that on the road this
morning.' She looked at Roderick. 'Do women
driving fast cars bring out your macho instincts?'

He smiled and shook his head. 'Being macho is
for guys who need to prove something. I may have
been macho at eighteen, but that was a long time
ago.'

He had all the right answers, she thought. But did they express his real feelings, or was it merely that he knew how to put himself over, to say the things that people wanted to hear and which would help him to achieve his own ends?

Either way, it made no difference to her decision.

'Thank you.' She took the glass from the salver Watson was offering and sipped the Campari while he replenished the men's glasses.

When he had left the room, she said, 'Has either of you had second thoughts about the deal you proposed?'

For once her grandfather was silent, leaving it to Roderick to say, 'Certainly not. Has talking it over with your best friend—which I gather was the reason for your visit—helped you to make up your mind?'

'Not really. As you told me the other day, other people's opinions are largely irrelevant. But I have made a decision.'

'Which is?'

'I think we should try being engaged and see how that works. Not for long . . . say, for two or three months.'

He smiled at her. 'I was going to suggest the same thing. To that end, while I was in London, I went to the bank and got out the family engagement ring. My mother received it from her mother-in-law, who had had it from my great-grandmother and so on back to the late-eighteenth century. By the time my parents went to Arizona, my mother's fingers were so thin that it was too loose to wear. She decided to leave it behind with one or two other family jewels.'

As he stood up he took from his pocket a worn leather ring-box. 'Of course, it may not appeal to you. If you don't like it you must say so.'

He opened the box and showed it to her; a marquise emerald surrounded by a cluster of diamonds.

Flower did not have to feign pleasure. 'It's beautiful,' she said sincerely.

'Shall I put it on?'

Before he could do so she had to remove the inexpensive dress-rings she was wearing on several fingers of her left hand. After putting them in her pocket, she held out her bare hand to him.

As Roderick slipped the Anstruther emerald on her third finger, her grandfather said delightedly, 'We must celebrate with champagne.' Beaming from ear to ear, he got up to press the bell to recall the butler.

Flower looked up into Roderick's eyes, searching for the slightest sign that this moment meant something more to him than the first step towards the achievement of his ambitions.

But, although she knew him to be capable of tenderness, or at least of simulating tenderness, at that moment his expression had never been more enigmatic.

CHAPTER SEVEN

THAT night Flower was reading in bed, in an effort to switch off thoughts which would keep her awake, when there was a knock at the door.

'Come in.'

Expecting to see her grandfather, she was surprised and disconcerted when Roderick walked into the room, closing the door behind him.

He was wearing the white towelling robe provided in all the guest bathrooms and had obviously just had a shower.

He came swiftly to the bedside, sat down, and took the book from her hands and put it aside on the night-table.

The next moment she was in his arms and the question 'What do you want?' was superfluous. His embrace made it clear what he wanted.

At first the pleasure of being enfolded by strong arms and kissed by lips tasting faintly of toothpaste, while her other senses registered that his jaw was newly-shaved and his skin smelt deliciously of soap and some very light lemony aftershave, overwhelmed all other reactions.

For a minute or two her response was the instinctive yielding of a woman in the arms of a man she loved and desired as ardently as he desired her.

With one of her hands caught between them and pressed to the warm brown skin exposed by the loosely sashed terry bathrobe, she could feel the strong, faster than normal beating of his heart. Her own heartbeat matched it.

More than anything in the world she wanted to surrender completely to the rapturous sensations and longings his powerful body and ardent kisses aroused in her.

Subconsciously, she had been wanting this ever since the night she had panicked and run from the morning-room. She was ready and eager to make love; to experience at last the real thing, the fusion of heart, soul and flesh with a man she adored.

And then, as she felt his fingers starting to undo the buttons of her Italian pyjamas, she remembered that he didn't love her. As, with two buttons unfastened, his hand slipped inside the silk jacket, she broke off the kiss and said, breathlessly but firmly, 'No . . . no . . . definitely not.'

'But we're engaged now,' he said.

Her resistance seemed to amuse him, and no doubt it did seem absurd to fend him off when her face must show all too clearly that, whatever she might claim to the contrary, she wanted him in her bed as much as he wished to be there.

If his eyes glittered, so must hers. If his colour had risen, her cheeks must also be flushed.

'You're taking too much for granted. This isn't a normal engagement and I'm not going to sleep with you until we're married,' she told him.

He didn't argue with her. Instead he captured her hands and, lightly clasping her wrists, began to press soft little kisses all over her right hand, alternating kisses with playful bites. And while he did this his eyes caressed her half-exposed breasts, which she was unable to cover.

'Aren't you being a little silly?' he asked, lifting the hand she was trying to free and holding it against his cheek.

'No, I'm trying to be sensible,' she said unsteadily.

'Trying' was the operative word. It was almost impossible to maintain her defences when her fingertips touched his cheekbone and longed to stroke it and the way he was nibbling her knuckles made the blood rush through her veins like the surge of a flood-tide.

She lay back on the pillows she had piled behind her to read, her breath coming faster and faster, her insides melting and throbbing, every nerve in her body conspiring against her common sense and self-control.

From her teens she had sensed that, when the right man arrived, she would be capable of intense passion; but this was her first experience of losing control. Other men had gone further without ever giving her the feeling she had now; the feeling that, if she couldn't stop him, Roderick would bring her to the brink of total abandonment.

He let go of her hands and stood up. 'All right... if that's the way you want it. Goodnight, Flower. Sweet dreams.'

His eyes mocking, he bowed and walked out of the room.

Two days later, after Roderick had informed his godparents, his aunts and a few close friends, their engagement was announced in the three national newspapers likely to be read by the other people whom it would interest.

The next day Flower received a letter from
London, signed Mary Dorset. It was from one of
Roderick's aunts, a gracious expression of pleasure
that her nephew had found a girl to share his life,
and an invitation to a small family party to celebrate their engagement.

To Flower's secret relief—a feeling of which she
was ashamed—the date set for the party conflicted
with her grandfather's visit to Germany to inspect
some new bakery machinery.

She felt that meeting Roderick's relations would
be rather an ordeal on her own, doubly so with
Dodo there.

In the event, the aunts—the other two had trav-
elled from Scotland and Devon to meet her—were
less daunting than she had feared. The two who
were visiting London were both no-nonsense
countrywomen, running large houses and gardens
with little help and enjoying a break from the chores
which were their everyday lot.

Mrs Dorset, a widow remarried to a director of
one of London's grandest antiques and fine-arts
galleries, lived a different but no less busy life, including being mother and stepmother to seven
children, some grown-up, some still in their teens.

Flower received the impression that, far from
eyeing her critically, the aunts were not concerned
about Roderick's marriage being what their generation called a *mésalliance*. They had problems
enough with their own offspring without worrying
about a nephew whom, clearly, they regarded as
perfectly competent to run his life without advice
or interference from them.

After the party, Roderick, who had arranged to sleep at his aunt's house in Belgravia, escorted Flower to her flat.

Since the night he had come to her room at the manor he had gone to the other extreme, behaving as circumspectly as a Victorian man engaged to the shyest of virgins. He had not even kissed her properly, and she knew his restraint was deliberate, an exasperating revenge for her refusal to sleep with him.

'Wait for me, would you?' he said to the driver when the taxi drew up in the forecourt of the block of flats where she had an apartment.

Then, watched by the night-duty porter, he saw her to the open lift, where he gave her a chaste kiss on the forehead and one of his sardonic smiles before returning to the street.

A few days later, leaving Lucy with her grandparents, Andrew and Emily drove down to spend a weekend at the manor.

They arrived on Friday night, and on Saturday morning, knowing how her friend loved to browse in antique and junk shops, Flower took Emily on a tour of the shops in the area.

No sooner were they alone in the Ferrari than Flower asked, 'What do you think of him?'

'I think he's a dish...a darling. If Andrew didn't exist, and you hadn't seen him first, I could fall for Roderick myself. I don't know why you ever hesitated about snapping him up,' said Emily.

Her verdict was not surprising, as Roderick had exerted himself to be nice to Flower's friends. When they left the house, he and Andrew had been lingering over a late breakfast, talking as if they had known each other for years.

On Monday, when the Fairchilds were to depart, Roderick was also leaving; going back to the States to settle his affairs there. He would be away for a month before returning to England for good.

'I'm glad you like him.'

'How could anyone not?' Emily gave her a sideways glance. 'Before you made up your mind, did you take your brother's advice?'

'No...no, I didn't...we haven't...'

'Why ever not?' asked her friend in surprise.

'I...just feel it's better not to. He wanted to but I didn't.'

'Come off it, Flower,' said Emily, 'I bet you're longing to. He certainly is.'

'What makes you say that?'

'The way he looks at you. Several times last night, before and after dinner, I noticed him looking at you like a tiger at a gazelle. He's *ravenous* for you, sweetie. I took it for granted he'd be tiptoeing to your room after lights-out.'

'We're having an old-fashioned engagement. No hanky-panky until the honeymoon.'

'You amaze me. Andrew and I did the deed on my eighteenth birthday and whenever we had the chance from then until we were married. Why not? I must say I shall be glad when my bulge has deflated,' she added wistfully. 'It seems ages since I was able to lie on my tummy or make love without this——' she patted her distended belly—'coming between us. This time next year you may be in the same boat. Or are you going to wait for a bit? Until the heart clinic is up and running, as they say?'

'We haven't discussed having children, except in the general sense that we both want to have a large family.'

'Well, there's no hurry, is there? Anyway, I expect you'll have a full-time nanny and be less bogged down in the early months than I was with Lucy and will be again until this one is eating solids and out of nappies.'

'I haven't thought that far ahead,' said Flower. 'Actually, I should have preferred to keep our engagement unofficial. It's supposed to be a trial period. But both Dodo and Roderick insisted that it should be official, and Dodo has instructed his lawyers to draw up a marriage settlement. Seems medieval to me. As far as I'm concerned, marriage means pooling resources. What's mine is yours, and what's yours is mine, et cetera.'

'That's how we look at it too,' said Emily. 'But then I'm not an heiress. The only money I have is the little bit Granny left me and what I can make from freelance dealing. But that doesn't amount to much now. There are precious few bargains these days—in fact, not much worth buying at all.'

Nevertheless, although all the dealers they visited during the morning complained of the difficulty of keeping their premises stocked, Emily managed to spend most of the cash she had with her and was especially delighted to find a pair of old red and cream *toile de Jouy* curtains which she said she could sell at a profit to a specialist dealer in London.

'Unless when I get them home I find I can't bear to part with them. Sooner or later we shall have to move to a larger house and, although your grandfather would think me mad, I'd much rather have nicely faded handmade old curtains at my windows than new ones, even if we could afford them.'

They returned to the manor to find Andrew waiting to meet them in front of the house. As by then it was nearly lunchtime, neither of them thought it strange that he should be there.

But, as the car slowed to a halt and he came forwards to open the passenger-door and help his wife to climb out, he stopped her from starting to tell him about their successful morning by saying, with a worried expression, 'I'm afraid I have bad news. It's your grandfather, Flower. He's been taken ill...seriously ill. Thank God Roderick was here when it happened. If he hadn't been...' He left the sentence unfinished.

Flower sprang out of the car. 'Where is Dodo? Upstairs?'

'No, it happened soon after you left...a heart attack. While Roderick took emergency measures, Watson phoned for an ambulance. Roderick went to the hospital with Mr Dursley. He rang up a short time ago to say he was on his way back but not to wait for lunch. He also stressed that there is no point in your going to the hospital yet. The old boy's in intensive care and probably won't be allowed any visitors until he's out of danger.'

'But of course I must go. If Dodo is dying...if he asks for me...'

She would have jumped back into the car, but Andrew restrained her. 'You are to stay here until Roderick comes. He was very firm about that. Come into the house, both of you.'

'Tell us exactly what happened,' said Emily as he shepherded them indoors.

'You'd been gone about fifteen minutes. Roderick and I were just about to go out for a walk when Watson came to tell us Mr Dursley wasn't feeling well. He was in his study, complaining of discomfort in his chest, arms and neck. Apparently he'd been tugging at a drawer in his desk which had stuck. Roderick gave him a tablet—nitroglycerin, I think he said it was—to dissolve under his tongue. But it didn't make him feel better. He began to sweat and feel sick. To make matters worse, as the pain increased he panicked. If there hadn't been a doctor on the spot I don't know what would have happened. Roderick managed to pacify him, saying it might only be a bad attack of angina pectoris brought on by exertion after a large fatty breakfast.'

'I'm not really surprised,' said Flower. 'I've been expecting this to happen sooner or later. Where is he? Where was he taken?'

'To the coronary care unit at the new Princess of Wales hospital on the other side of the bypass,' said Andrew, who had noticed the striking new building on his way to the manor the day before. 'Luckily the ambulance got here very quickly.'

Ten anxious minutes later, Roderick returned, his face and manner reassuringly calm.

'How bad is it?' was Flower's first question. 'I should be there...even if he's unconscious. I couldn't bear it if he asked for me and I wasn't there.'

'They will let me know immediately if there's any change in his condition. For the moment he's been sedated to relieve his physical pain and also his mental distress. As heart patients often are, he was very frightened, poor old chap,' Roderick told her. 'He's had what is technically known as a myocardial infarction which, in simple terms, means the death of a piece of the heart muscle caused by restricted or obstructed blood-flow. But he's having the best possible treatment and I think he should pull through. Both President Eisenhower and President Johnson had several heart attacks before, during and after their presidencies. It didn't stop them carrying what is arguably the heaviest load of responsibility in the Western world.'

His mention of responsibility made her give an exclamation of dismay as she realised that her brother, who must now shoulder all her grandfather's responsibilities, knew nothing of what had happened.

'I must call Stephen,' she said.

'I've already spoken to him,' Roderick told her. 'He knows he's fully in charge now and it may be the chance he's needed to show your grandfather that he can cope on his own. At this stage it's impossible to say whether Mr Dursley will make a full recovery, but at best it's going to be some weeks before he can take over the reins again.'

After insisting that, even if she wasn't hungry, she must eat an adequate lunch, Roderick drove her to the hospital.

On the way he prepared her for the sight of her grandfather with a drip-feed in his arm, electro-cardiographic equipment strapped to his chest and possibly other attachments such as a catheter and oxygen mask.

'It's important that you appear to be calm and confident,' he warned her. 'For the first few days its essential for cardiac patients not to be subjected to any additional stress such as tearful friends and relations.'

'I won't cry,' she assured him.

Nevertheless the room in the intensive care unit where Abel Dursley was lying at the centre of a web of tubes and wires, the action of his damaged heart under constant surveillance in a nearby monitoring-room, might have upset her had she not been prepared for its stark spaceship atmosphere.

Later, on the way home from the hospital, Roderick said, 'There's a strong possibility that your grandfather's illness has its origins in his childhood. Studies show that many diseases stem from a poor start in life. Also he's what we call an "A type" personality; someone engaged in a perpetual struggle to be more successful, who can't relax and take it easy, who never makes time to "stand and stare". But maybe he will from now on. Sometimes, after a heart attack, people realise for the first time what life is about... what's important and what isn't.'

He sounded so wise, thought Flower. But, if he knew the difference between important and unimportant things, what was he doing marrying a girl he wasn't in love with for her money?

When the electronically operated gates of the manor had opened for them and they were approaching the house, she said, 'What's happened would have been much more upsetting if you hadn't been here. I'm very grateful to you, Roderick. Both for handling the emergency this morning and for explaining the treatment and after-effects. The staff at the hospital obviously haven't got time to translate all the technical terms into layman's language.'

'I'm glad I was here to help—and I'll stay till he's out of the wood. I'll call the airline and cancel tomorrow's flight.'

'Can you do that? Won't it be very inconvenient?'

'It's a question of priorities. Right now I think you need someone to see you through this unexpected crisis. Not because you couldn't cope alone. I'm sure you could if you had to. But I wouldn't be happy leaving you on your own at a time like this.'

'Thank you. I would be glad to have someone with me until Dodo's off the danger-list.' She kept her tone unemotional, but inside she was deeply affected by his understanding and kindness.

But she didn't delude herself that his motives for staying were those of most newly engaged men. It was his training as a doctor and his vested interest in her welfare, not any deep personal feeling, which made him supportive.

That evening Stephen and Sharon joined them for supper. Stephen had been to the hospital on his way home from the works, but his grandfather had been sleeping.

'I just hope to goodness I can handle it,' her brother said anxiously when they had a few minutes alone together.

'Of course you can,' Flower answered with more assurance than she felt inwardly. 'It may be that, even if Dodo recovers, he will have to retire. Whatever happens, he's not going to be on your back for at least a month, perhaps longer.'

Stephen said, 'I know it's a rotten thing to say, but even coming round tonight without him here is better. I don't want him to die. But sometimes I wish I'd run away...emigrated...gone somewhere where I didn't have to live in his shadow.'

'If you had you wouldn't have met Sharon.'

'That's true. Without her I couldn't have stood these last two years. He's been making my life a misery. Let's hope that, when he comes out—if he comes out—he won't turn nasty with you. He won't take kindly to being an invalid, you know.'

Until then it had not struck her that, if her grandfather survived but made only a partial recovery, he would have to remain at the manor after her marriage. She wondered if Roderick had considered that possibility. She felt sure he would never tolerate any interference in the way his clinic was run. Her spirits sank at the thought of being a buffer between them.

She said, 'I'll cross that bridge when I come to it. Anyway, now is your chance to show what you can do when you're not being harassed.'

Her brother and his wife did not stay late. Having seen them off, Flower remained standing on the sweep, watching the flicker of the car's tail-lights as they drove down the long beech-lined drive.

She was lost in thought when the gravel behind her crunched and Roderick said, 'To make certain you get a good night's sleep, I prescribe a brisk walk as far as the gates and back. I'll come with you.' He was holding an old mackintosh she kept in the lobby leading to the downstairs cloakroom, waiting for her to put her arms in the sleeves.

In silence they followed the car down the moonlit drive and saw its lights disappear as it turned on to the minor road which passed the gates.

Flower had changed for supper, but only into a Kaffe Fassett sweater, clean jeans and comfortable leather moccasins. But, even in flat heels, she could only just keep up with the pace he was setting.

As they turned at the gate he said, 'When we get back I want you to have a warm bath and then drink a cup of hot milk—which I've asked Watson to organise—with some calcium tablets I'll give you. You'll sleep well and wake up refreshed, ready to cope with tomorrow.'

'You don't believe in sleeping-tablets, I gather?'

'Definitely not. You don't take them, do you?'

'Everyone else in my family does, but I've never needed them.'

'No one needs them. We all have sleepless nights occasionally, but chronic insomnia is a fairly rare condition. Sedatives have their uses, as in your grandfather's present condition, but they aren't the best way to correct poor sleeping habits.'

She was tempted to confide that what might keep her awake tonight was the worry Stephen had added to her existing anxieties.

However, after vacillating for a few minutes, she decided to keep it to herself.

'Good morning. Did my prescription work?' Roderick asked her when she entered the dining-room to find him the first one there.

'Perfectly, thank you. I slept like a log until my alarm clock buzzed.'

'Good. I'm glad to hear it.' He had risen to draw out a chair for her. As she seated herself, he added, 'Of course, the simplest and best method of en-suring sound sleep is to make love.' He resumed his place alongside her. 'But that isn't always possible or, in your case, acceptable.'

Flower felt a wash of hot colour suffuse her face and neck. When she would have averted her face, in an attempt to hide it, he took hold of her chin and forced her to meet his eyes.

'You're always a delight to the eye, Flower, but particularly so at the moment,' he told her. 'I must make it happen more often...the blush and the angry sparkle.'

He was bending his head towards hers when the door opened and they were joined by the others.

Unhurriedly Roderick let his hand fall and rose to say good morning to Emily and Andrew.

After breakfast he rang the hospital.

'Your grandfather's had a good night and is holding his own,' he reported. 'Later today the results of tests should show how much of his heart has been damaged.'

Three days later, Abel was transferred to an ordinary room in the hospital, and ten days after his heart attack he was allowed to go home to follow an eight-week programme of rehabilitation under the supervision of a specially trained therapist. At his insistence, a night-nurse was engaged to be on call if he felt ill in the night.

The day after Abel's discharge, Roderick returned to America to wind up his affairs there.

Flower felt curiously lost without him. The heart attack seemed to have changed her grandfather's personality. Far from being impatient to resume control of his business, he appeared to have lost interest in it and to be obsessed by his health. At the same time he was dissatisfied with the restricted diet prescribed for him, bored by inactivity yet reluctant to take the gentle exercise which would aid his recovery.

His mood-swings were hard to handle, but Flower devoted herself to helping him overcome the problems of his convalescence.

It was a difficult time, which would have been made easier by more frequent contact with

Roderick. But it had been agreed that he would call twice a week and she had to be content with these brief and somewhat stilted transatlantic calls.

One evening her grandfather said to her, 'I've made a good recovery and they say there's no reason why, if I take things a bit easier, I shouldn't go on for years. But they're making no guarantees. They know—and I know—I could snuff it any time.'

'That applies to everyone, Dodo. I'm sure if you do as they tell you——'

'If I've got to live like an invalid, I'd just as soon *not* make old bones. But there is one weight on my mind which doesn't need to be there, and I'll stand a better chance without it.'

'What's that?'

'Your future, that's what, lass, I want to see you and Rod married and settled down. There's no point in any more shilly-shallying. The pair of you couldn't be better suited, in my opinion. The sooner you're wed the easier my mind will be.'

'But it's barely a month since we met,' she protested. 'We agreed to wait for two or three months.'

'Aye, but that was before my old ticker started playing up. If it hadn't been for Rod being with me when I was taken bad, I might not be here today. It'd ease my mind to know, if it happened again, that you'd got a good 'un taking care of you.'

'I'm quite capable of taking care of myself, Dodo.'

'So you say, but I'd sooner see you safely married. You've a headstrong streak in you, Flower. You need a strong hand to guide you and, for all his smooth upper-crust ways, Rod's got what it takes. He's like me . . . he's shrewd and he's tough.'

If her grandfather had spoken in this vein before his illness, Flower would have rebutted vigorously the suggestion that she needed looking after. Now she was reluctant to argue with him for fear of the effect on his heart if he became incensed, as he always had when anyone had dared to disagree with him and no doubt still would if opposed.

'I only wish your brother was a bit more like him,' he went on. 'Stephen's a disappointment to me. But you've always been my favourite and, once the knot's tied and your future is settled, I shan't fret too much about your brother's shortcomings.'

'Roderick may not agree to reducing the agreed time,' she said.

'He will,' her grandfather said confidently. 'It was you who insisted on waiting two or three months, not him. Once he'd made up his mind, he'd have married you the next day if you'd been willing.'

'But I wasn't... and I'm still not keen to rush things.'

'It wasn't necessary before and it may not be necessary now. With luck, I'll live to see you the mother of two or three bonny youngsters. But I can't count on that. So, if you want to please me, you'll tell Roderick you've changed your mind and are ready to wed him immediately. I've seen the way he looks at you. You won't find him backing off. He'll be as pleased as a dog with two tails.'

Later, thinking over Abel's mandate—for that was what it was, not a plea, not a hopeful request—Flower knew that, deep down, it made no difference to her whether she and Roderick were married now or later.

She had been committed to him within hours of their meeting. For better or worse, she was his. But whether their marriage would be happy and lasting was anyone's guess.

Roderick was due to ring up that night. When he did, the first thing he said was that he would be seeing her at the weekend. He had done all that was necessary, and any remaining loose ends could be handled by others on his behalf.

Thrilled at the thought of seeing him so much sooner than she had anticipated, Flower offered to meet him at Heathrow, but he wouldn't hear of it.

It was mid-afternoon when he arrived back at the manor. Flower longed to welcome him with outstretched arms, but restrained herself, and Roderick's greeting was a social kiss on her cheek.

Over tea in the library, when she told him what Abel wanted, his reaction was not the eager agreement her grandfather had forecast.

'I have no objection, but how do you feel about it?' he asked, his manner guarded.

'Dodo has set his heart on it and he doesn't take kindly to opposition. Given a choice between pleasing or upsetting him, I would rather—within reason—please him.'

'Naturally, but I don't think you should let him pressure you into anything you're not sure about,' was his comment.

She was faintly piqued by his lack of enthusiasm.

'Dodo thought *you* would jump at the idea. He's under the impression you can't wait to marry me.'

'He's right.'

'You don't *sound* very eager.'

'On the contrary, I demonstrated my eagerness on the night we became engaged. However, as it wasn't mutual, I've done my best to keep my feelings under hatches.'

The reminder of his visit to her room made her colour rise, and it deepened even more when he added, 'Was that a misjudgement? Should I have been more persistent?'

Remembering the feelings he had aroused in her that night, she had a powerful longing to feel his arms round her, his mouth on hers. But she wasn't going to tell him that.

It seemed that he didn't need telling. Before she could think of an answer he sprang to his feet and hauled her against him.

Looking down at her upturned face, he said, 'I want you, Flower. Make no mistake about that. The sooner you're mine, the better I'll like it.'

And then he demonstrated his impatience with a kiss which left her limp and shaken, clutching at him for support in case he should let go as abruptly as he had seized her.

'Are you convinced or would you like further proof?' he asked huskily as she opened her eyes.

Flower, who for a few moments had felt that every bone in her body had melted in the furnace-blast of that passionate kiss, said unsteadily, 'I'm convinced.'

'Good. But you haven't answered my question. Has my restraint been unnecessary? Has your attitude changed?'

She withdrew from his arms and, rather to her disappointment, he didn't try to prevent her.

'Only to the extent that, if you want it and Dodo wants it, I'm prepared to marry you as soon as it can be arranged.'

Roderick's mouth twisted in a mocking grimace. 'If I believed that tepid concession was the true measure of your feelings I'd call the whole thing off. But I don't. You want me as much as I want you, but for some reason you can't bring yourself to admit it. Well, I can wait.'

His eyes narrowed, raking her slender form from her face to her feet and back again, before he said, 'Because I have a feeling that, when you do finally let your hair down, it's going to be worth the wait. You've kept me at arm's length a long time and if that's the way you want it, or pretend you want it, I'll stay there until we're officially man and wife. But once we are...' he paused, his gaze like a blue flame '...once we are,' he repeated, 'that "touch me not" sign is going to be dumped overboard...and all inhibitions with it.'

CHAPTER EIGHT

RODERICK'S ultimatum echoed in Flower's mind often in the days that followed. Each time she remembered it, a little shiver of mingled excitement and nervousness ran through her.

Why had he added that rider about inhibitions? Did he think it was prudishness which had made her send him away on the night of their engagement? Yet once he had made a remark suggesting he thought she'd had numerous lovers.

Something which troubled her deeply was the possibility that the hunger he had demonstrated in that cataclysmic kiss at teatime on the day he'd come back might swiftly burn itself out. Without love, how was she going to hold him once her body lost its novelty for him?

Since his return to England he had had little or no contact with the local people he would have mixed with had his father and mother remained at the manor. But once he had reclaimed his heritage he would inevitably be drawn back into the circles his parents had moved in. Would he then begin to regret his marriage to 'Flour' Dursley, as she had been unkindly dubbed by a snobbish girl in her first year at boarding-school? Would he begin to wish he had married a girl of his own kind?

Her misgivings grew worse as the expedited date of the wedding drew nearer. She had never visualised being married in a register office. Her grandfather, now making a rapid improvement, would have liked to make the wedding as big a splash as possible. He was not pleased that Roderick was implacably opposed to a large society wedding involving many complex and time-consuming arrangements. Roderick's preference was for a civil ceremony: brief, businesslike and, if possible, unpublicised.

Flower herself would have liked to compromise with a small, quiet wedding in the parish church a mile from the manor. But she could see that, given an inch, there would be no stopping Abel from taking the proverbial mile.

Rather than give him the chance to expand a wedding with about twenty guests into one with two hundred or more, it was better to have none at all, other than the necessary witnesses.

Even though she knew a register-office wedding would take only a few minutes, it would still be a momentous event and she gave considerable thought to what to wear for the occasion.

Nothing in her existing wardrobe was suitable and, with no clear idea of the kind of garment she was looking for, she spent a day shopping in London. What Roderick would think of her choice when he saw it she had no idea. Probably her bridal outfit was a matter of indifference to him.

Flower had been Emily's bridesmaid. From her place behind her white-clad tulle-veiled friend she had seen, and would never forget, Andrew Fairchild's expression when he'd seen his bride coming up the aisle on her father's arm. But Andrew, although he had known Emily all his life and, while she was growing up, had treated her like a sister, had by that time been deeply in love with her.

Roderick was a man of a different stamp: realistic, practical, unsentimental. Andrew, she felt certain, would always remember how ravishing Emily had looked in her rustling Victorian-style crinoline of white silk taffeta, the family tiara lent by Andrew's mother sparkling on her hair, her eyes bright with excitement and happiness behind the misty meshes of her veil.

Fifty years on, when they were both in their seventies, their wedding-day would be a treasured memory.

Although Flower had agreed to the brief formalities in front of the local superintendent registrar, her romantic heart ached a little because for her there would be no garlanded church, no organ and choir, no radiant walk down the aisle on her bridegroom's arm, smiling at friends and relations in morning suits and pretty hats.

The afternoon before the wedding, she was writing to thank Emily's parents for their present when Watson came to inform her that a Mrs Meltzer wished to see her.

'Mrs Meltzer?' she said blankly.

'An American lady, Miss Dursley. She first asked to see Sir Roderick. When I told her he was not at home she asked for you.'

'Show her into the drawing-room. I'll be down in a few minutes.'

Watson said, 'It would appear that Mrs Meltzer is expecting to stay here. She has two suitcases with her and has dismissed her taxi. Is it possible that Sir Roderick has invited her to the wedding and forgotten to mention it? He has a great deal on his mind at present.'

'That's true, but he isn't the kind of person who forgets things... certainly not the arrival of a guest,' said Flower. 'There must be some other explanation. Tell her I won't keep her waiting long.'

As the butler withdrew she completed the sentence she had been writing and rose from her desk, leaving the letter to be finished later.

She had hoped that Emily and Andrew would be at the wedding, but their baby—a boy—had been born two days ago and her friend could not come. It was a big disappointment.

It was difficult to judge the age of the woman who was waiting for her in the drawing-room.

She had the smooth flawless skin possessed by some girls of eighteen, as well as the sparkling eyes and shining hair of the very young. But in other respects her appearance was that of someone at least in her late twenties and possibly in her early thirties.

She was plainly yet elegantly dressed in grey trousers, a wool jacket, checked with black and grey on camel, and a turtle-necked camel sweater. Gold hoop earrings and a gold lapel-pin were discreetly stylish finishing touches to an outfit which was obviously part of a carefully chosen mix-and-match wardrobe of classic separates.

A short cap of reddish-brown hair framed a pleasant, intelligent face. Her bright, friendly eyes were the colour of cream sherry. She appeared to be wearing no make-up but, with her remarkable skin and the natural pinkness of her lips, did not look dowdy without it.

Flower had never met anyone—except Roderick—who emanated health and vitality to the same extent as Mrs Meltzer. She looked as if she wouldn't know what it was to be tired, never caught a cold, and never, ever had off-days.

At the same time there was something in her face which conflicted with her air of physical well-being. Any intuitive person, on meeting her, would wonder if she had been through some kind of spiritual ordeal.

'How do you do, Miss Dursley?' Her smile parted the full pink lips to reveal rather large but otherwise perfect teeth. 'I'm Kimberley Meltzer. My husband George was Roderick's best friend. I'm sure Roderick has told you about him. The three of us were very close until George was killed in an automobile accident.'

So that was it. She had lost her husband. Flower remembered Roderick talking about them the morning Mrs Wood had fallen off a chair in the pantry and he had given her first aid.

She said, 'Yes, he has. You're a nutritionist, I believe.'

'That's right. I hope you'll forgive me for descending on you without warning,' the American went on. 'I'm not usually impulsive, and I meant to spend my vacation with my parents. But I really wasn't in the mood for two weeks in Florida and suddenly I couldn't resist my curiosity to see this lovely old house and to meet Roderick's fiancée.'

'You're very welcome, Mrs Meltzer,' said Flower, although privately she thought it most peculiar to arrive, without notice, the day before the wedding.

Perhaps, now she came to think of it, it was rather odd that Roderick hadn't invited Kimberley Meltzer to come to it. But he might have felt that a wedding would be an upsetting occasion for a young widow. It was possible that, preoccupied as he was with plans for the clinic, he might even have neglected to tell her that his wedding had been put forward.

To find out if her visitor knew that by this time tomorrow he would he starting his honeymoon, Flower said, 'Have you other friends in England? Are you planning a round of visits?'

'Why, no, I was planning to stay here...if it's convenient? I'm very interested in the clinic Roderick is setting up. It was I who got him interested in the connection between junk food and delinquent behaviour, you know.'

'Oh, really? I'm sure he'll be delighted to see you, and of course you're welcome to stay as long as you like. But perhaps you don't realise that we shan't be here after tomorrow.'

'You won't? Oh, that's too bad. Where are you going?'

'To an island in the Caribbean. We'll be on our honeymoon.'

'Your honeymoon!' Kimberley exclaimed. 'I had no idea you were getting married so soon. Not till next year, that was what Roderick said.'

'We've had a change of plan...partly because my grandfather had a heart attack recently and he wanted the wedding brought forward in case he should have another.'

'I see. But is that wise? I mean...you've known each other such a short time.' The nutritionist did not hide her dismay at Flower's announcement.

At that moment Watson and John arrived with the tea things, and Flower gave instructions for her uninvited guest's luggage to be taken up to the bedroom described in the inventory as the Chinese room because it contained two beautiful Chinese screens.

When the butler and footman had withdrawn and Flower was pouring out tea, Kimberley said, 'This has been quite a shock.'

'It's a pity you didn't ring up before coming.'

'I guess so... but why didn't Roderick call me... tell me?'

'He's been busy setting in motion the conversion of part of the house into a clinic. It's a complex project and he wanted to get things moving before going away.'

'It's not like him to rush into things. I know him very well. He's not a man who acts impetuously... rashly.' Kimberley's tone sounded faintly accusing, as if she suspected Flower of putting undue pressure on him.

Suddenly Flower remembered how, when Roderick had told her about his friend George, she had formed the impression that his sympathy and affection for George's widow might have developed into something stronger than friendship.

She had not thought much more about it. But now the American's aghast reaction to the news of his wedding made her wonder afresh if, before coming back to England, he had given Kimberley cause to believe their future lay together.

For the next half an hour, she and Kimberley made rather stilted conversation. Then she took the other woman upstairs to the room prepared for her and suggested that, as Roderick was unlikely to be back for some time, she might like to bath and rest until it was time for drinks before dinner.

Kimberley agreed to this suggestion. Flower went back to her own room, feeling guilty because she expected Roderick to reappear at about half-past five, but she didn't want him dashing upstairs to greet the American in private. She wanted to be present when they met.

For the first time in her life she was jealous. It was an emotion she had always despised and it worried her to find herself feeling it, perhaps without cause.

Roderick returned to the manor at twenty to six. She saw him drive up from her window and guessed he would go to his room for a shower and to watch the news on TV before coming down to join her and Dodo in the drawing-room at a quarter to seven.

Abel's doctor had not insisted on total abstinence. Her grandfather was allowed two drinks before dinner and two glasses of wine with the meal. She had poured him a single brandy and topped it up with diet soda when they were joined by Roderick.

After a few minutes' conversation, Flower said, 'While you were out you had a visitor.'

He raised an eyebrow. 'Who was it?'

'She should be down any time now. She's staying here. It's your American friend...Kimberley Meltzer.'

'She's *here*?' For an instant he looked as dumbfounded as Kimberley had when told of tomorrow's wedding.

Before he had recovered from his surprise the door opened and Kimberley herself walked in. She had changed into a printed silk dress with a scarf collar tied in a bow at one side of her neck.

But Flower didn't take in any other details because she was watching Roderick closely.

'Kim!' he exclaimed before striding towards her, arms wide.

Watching them embrace didn't make Flower any wiser about the nature of their relationship from his point of view. But the glow on Kimberley's face as she went into his outstretched arms, and the way she closed her eyes when he gave her a brief but close hug, made it clear she was *very* fond of him.

'Who's this?' Abel asked gruffly, looking put out.

Briefly Flower explained, and a moment later Roderick brought her over and introduced her.

The evening that followed was an awkward one. Kimberley seemed to feel that it was her social duty not to allow any lulls in the conversation, and Abel was at his most taciturn. He had never enjoyed the company of women, most of whom he regarded as fools, and his illness had accentuated his quirks. He had no inclination to be an affable host and responded with gruff monosyllables to efforts to include him in the table talk.

At the end of the meal he announced that he was going to bed and asked Flower to give her his arm as if he needed assistance to get there.

'What the hell is that silly bitch doing here?' he demanded loudly as they crossed the hall.

'Hush, Dodo... they're old friends.'

'Doesn't give her the right to turn up here un-invited. She's got her eye on him if you ask me,' Abel said crossly. 'Well, she's too late. He's spoken for. You'd better get back in there and keep an eye on her.'

But when Flower returned to the drawing-room, she said, 'I'm sure you two have masses to talk about, so if you'll excuse me, Kim, I'm going to have an early night.'

'Of course...what a good idea,' the other woman said brightly. 'I won't keep Roderick up too late but, as you say, we do have a lot to talk about.'

'Goodnight, Roderick.' Flower did not offer her cheek to him.

'Goodnight.'

His response was as formal as if they were mere acquaintances, not a man and woman who tomorrow morning were entering into what should be a lifelong contract; and who tomorrow night would be sharing a bridal bed.

Because of the nature of the occasion there was little point in the bride and groom arriving at the register office separately. But, although she was to drive there with her bridegroom as well as her grandfather—and now, presumably, with Kim in the car as well—Flower chose to have breakfast in her bedroom and not to join the others until a few minutes before they were due to set out.

As she walked slowly down the staircase she could hear their voices below her, or rather her grandfather's voice. He was telling Roderick the history of his watch, a gold hunter presented to his grandfather at the end of fifty years' service with a firm in the industrial Midlands, the region round Birmingham and Wolverhampton at that time known as the Black Country because so much of it was blackened by uncontrolled smoke from the chimneys of many factories.

'He treasured this watch, did my poor old gaffer,' she heard Abel saying. 'And so do I, but for a different reason. I was fourteen years old when he left it to me, and I made up my mind I wasn't going to waste my life working for someone else's benefit. At the end of the day I was going to have more to show than the rotten little pension they gave him and a two-guinea watch. It's worth a lot more today, of course. I dare say a watch like this would set you back two hundred quid now. But that was its value in his time.'

Flower paused at a turn in the stairs and saw Roderick looking down at her grandfather with no sign of the boredom he was probably feeling. He had on a grey worsted suit with a cream shirt and cream and grey tie, and he looked very tall and debonair at the side of the short, obese man whose tailor could never disguise his short neck and ungainly girth.

'Flower ought to be down here by now,' said her grandfather.

'Here I am, Dodo.' She moved down the stairs, avoiding the eyes of the man to whom, within the hour, she would be bound if not forever at least for some time to come.

It pained her to think on her wedding-day that her marriage might not be for life. But how could she feel that certainty when there was no love on Roderick's side?

'Where's your coat?' Abel demanded.

Clearly he was not impressed by her simple cream chiffon dress.

'I shan't need a coat.'

She had briefly considered wearing the full-length pale cashmere coat which had been one of his many extravagant presents. But she had rejected the idea on the grounds that the coat wasn't suitable for such a quiet wedding. For the same reason she was wearing no jewellery other than small pearl earrings and her three gold bangles.

'It's a very mild morning,' said Roderick, who had evidently been for his usual run before breakfast.

He took a small case, about the size of her calculator, from his pocket.

'Perhaps you won't want to wear this today, Flower, but I'd like you to have it now. It's one of the few family jewels to survive my grandfather's depredations.'

He opened the case and lifted, by its chain, a heavy green and gold pendant. As he handed it to her she saw that the brilliant colour came from a piece of malachite on which was superimposed an exquisitely detailed gold tracery. The design was a stylised tree.

'It's beautiful. Is it Russian?' For the first time she met his eyes.

'That's clever of you...yes, it is. It's supposed to have been given to one of my ancestors by Catherine the Great, but I'm inclined to doubt that story. How did you know where it came from?'

'By the malachite and the design. I think it's the singing tree, isn't it?'

'I've never heard of the singing tree. Tell me about it.'

'Not now. It's time we were off,' said Abel. 'Where's that American got to? I hope she's not going to keep us waiting.'

'Will you put it on for me, please?' Flower handed the jewel to Roderick and turned her back.

He lifted it over her head and the smooth gold back of the pendant struck her lightly at the base of the throat before sliding down inside the Vneckline of her dress to lie between her breasts. It felt cold against her skin. She fished it out, conscious of Roderick's fingers brushing the nape of her neck.

The thought that in a few hours' time he would unfasten the clasp and remove not only the pendant but everything else she was wearing sent a tingle shivering down her spine. She didn't think he would wait until tonight to make love to her. Possibly it would happen as soon as they reached her flat, where they were spending one night before flying to the Caribbean for two weeks in the sun.

Would it be the ecstatic experience she longed for, the redeeming feature of a marriage lacking all the other harmonies which should exist between a husband and wife?

The fear that it might prove disappointing made her very nervous. If their sexual relationship was no good, their marriage was doomed from the beginning.

In the car he sat in front with the chauffeur and she in the back with her grandfather, fingering the pendant and thinking about the singing tree which, according to an old Russian folk tale, grew on an island in the middle of a huge lake. Anyone who discovered it would find everything they had ever wanted near it.

Had Roderick known the significance of the design, and had he been in love with her, the pendant would have been a perfect wedding present.

CHAPTER NINE

STEPHEN and Sharon, as their witnesses, were waiting for them at the register office. In spite of Flower's injunction not to dress up too much, her sister-in-law was wearing a glittery knitted dress under a shadow-dyed fox jacket and a white felt fez with a big gold tassel bobbing above her left ear.

Roderick introduced them to Kim, who was wearing another neat classic silk dress, or the material might have been a crease-proof synthetic. But, whatever it was, she had the impeccable grooming, the band-box look for which American women were famous.

A vase of carnations stood on the registrar's desk, but otherwise his room, with its cream-painted walls and mottled vinyl floor-tiles, was as soulless as most local government offices.

Her throat thick with sudden tears, Flower listened to Roderick saying briskly, 'I do solemnly declare that I know not of any lawful impediment why I Roderick Charles Paget Anstruther may not be joined in matrimony to Flower Jane Dursley. I call upon these persons here present to witness that I, Roderick Charles Paget Anstruther, do take thee, Flower Jane Dursley, to be my lawful wedded wife.'

Then it was her turn to say the words, after which Roderick produced the wedding ring.

She had forgotten to transfer her engagement ring to her other hand. Without giving her a chance to

remedy the oversight, he slipped the plain gold ring
on her finger above the Anstruther emerald so that,
before the day was out, she would have to take them
off and exchange them.

Fortunately she wasn't superstitious, but Sharon
was. Flower heard the other girl's indrawn gasp of
dismay as she saw what had happened. From now
on Sharon would be convinced their marriage
wouldn't prosper. And perhaps she would be right,
although not for that reason.

For the last time Flower signed her maiden name.
The registrar offered them his congratulations and
good wishes. The others, including Kim, hugged
and kissed her and, predictably, Sharon giggled and
asked, 'How does it feel to be Lady Anstruther?'

Flower responded with an embarrassed smile. She
felt like weeping.

Perhaps to a couple in love this short down-to-
earth form of marriage was as memorable as any
other. But to her it had emphasised the businesslike
nature of the bond they had made.

On the way back to the manor her grandfather
and Kim went in Stephen's car, leaving the back of
the Rolls-Royce to the bride and groom.

'I like your dress,' said Roderick.

'Thank you.'

To her surprise, he took her right hand in his and
raised it to his lips for a quick light kiss.

'You were nervous, weren't you?'

'Yes,' she admitted. 'Weren't you... inwardly?'

'No, not at all.'

He continued to hold her hand loosely, stroking
the side of her forefinger with his thumb. She suspected that, instead of having lunch at the manor,
he would have preferred to drive directly to London.

In some ways she would have preferred that arrangement herself. She wasn't hungry and a
wedding breakfast for only six people promised to
be heavy going. What was there to talk about?

Watson had champagne waiting for them. As he
offered the tray to the bridal couple he made a brief
speech of congratulation on behalf of the staff.

Two hours later, when it was time to leave in the
Ferrari, Flower realised she had not eaten enough
to counterbalance the effect of four or five glasses
of champagne.

Not wanting to draw attention to the fact that
her secret stresses had made her drink more than
was wise when she had no appetite, she climbed
into the passenger-seat, prepared to make a joking
remark about male prerogatives if Roderick showed
surprise.

He, she felt sure, was totally clear-headed. Not
only was he more accustomed to alcohol, but he
had done full justice to the luncheon she had ordered. She had watched him enjoying the meal and
making himself pleasant to his new in-laws while
she'd pushed the food round her plate and hoped
the wine would make her cheerful and carefree.

To some extent it had. But it had also made her
slightly woozy, and she knew she lacked the con-
centration to drive a fast car on the motorway.

For the first half-hour of the journey they listened
to music on the radio and exchanged few remarks.

Then, nearing a service area, he moved from the
outer lane to the inner lane and, at the slip road,
turned off. Having parked, he surprised her by
producing a vacuum flask.

'I asked Watson to lay on tea and biscuits. I suspect you didn't have a decent breakfast and you ate like a bird at lunch,' he said.

The weak tea she had at home—in the motorway cafeteria it would have been a strong brown brew—accompanied by a plain biscuit was precisely what Flower had been longing for.

She had begun to have a headache. Not a bad one. A slight dull ache in her temples.

Roderick seemed to know about that, too. As she was sipping the tea he dropped two tablets on to her lap.

'How did you know I had a headache?' she asked.

'A poor night's sleep...tension...alcohol. It was inevitable,' he said drily.

She made no comment on his assumption that she hadn't slept well. He was right. Had he slept soundly? she wondered.

After two cups of tea and several biscuits she began to feel better. Or was it his thoughtful kindness which had wrought the cure? By the time they were on the outskirts of London the headache had gone.

However, as they crossed the Thames the tension returned. Her insides began to knot with mingled apprehension and excitement. Out of the corner of her eye she watched the economical movements with which he controlled the powerful car. Was he equally adept at making love? Or were all the dreams of tenderness and passion she had woven round Piers Anstruther about to be shattered by the flesh and blood man who was so extraordinarily like him?

Very soon they were gliding down the ramp to
the basement garage where each apartment had a
numbered parking space. For security reasons there
was no lift service between the basement and the
flats. Everyone entering the garage had to use the
stairs to the ground floor, which was under round-
the-clock surveillance by a hall porter.

Flower was on friendly terms with the two retired policemen who performed this duty. One of
them was a voracious reader and she supplied him
with many of the paperbacks he devoured while on
night duty. She knew the names of all their grand-
children and was shown the latest photographs of
them.

'Hello, Miss Dursley. Nice dry weather you've
brought with you this time,' said Mr Taylor, the
day porter, as she and Roderick walked through
the lobby.

She smiled and nodded. 'But I'm not Miss
Dursley any more, Mr Taylor. This is my husband.
We were married this morning.'

'You don't say? That is a surprise. Mrs
Brewer——' referring to her cleaner—'didn't let on
you were getting married, miss...madam, I should
say.'

'She doesn't know yet. We wanted to keep it very
quiet. We're just here for one night before going
on our honeymoon.'

'Well, congratulations, sir. You don't need me
to tell you that your wife is one of the nicest young
ladies it's ever been my pleasure to meet,' said the
porter.

'Thank you. I agree,' Roderick said smoothly.

Mr Taylor opened the book in which incoming messages and special arrangements were noted. 'What is the name, sir?'

Roderick produced a card and laid it on the desk. Then, a hand under Flower's elbow, he steered her to the lift, which was being vacated by a couple coming down from an upper floor.

Her suitcase, containing her small sun-and-sea trousseau, was still in the car, as was his case. All he was carrying was a small leather pack which presumably contained his shaving gear. Evidently he didn't expect to need pyjamas or a dressing-gown tonight. Her night-clothes, and fresh underthings to put on tomorrow, were already in the flat, left there on her previous visit.

A covert glance at her watch showed that it was now half-past five. They had booked a table for eight at a very good Italian restaurant a few minutes' walk from the apartments. They had two and a half hours to fill before going out to dine, and clearly they weren't going to fill it by making conversation or watching television.

Had they been normal newly-weds, leaping straight into bed would have been natural and easy. In the circumstances she found the situation fraught with awkwardness, and now regretted her refusal to let him make love to her during their engagement.

Roderick, however, seemed wholly at ease as he unlocked the door with the key she had had cut for him, and followed her through the small hall and into the sitting-room.

But it was different for him. Presumably he was accustomed to going to bed with women he desired but did not love. If she proved a disappointing partner, the let-down would not be as total for him as for her. As time went on he would undoubtedly stray. He had not promised her fidelity, either formally at their wedding or privately. But for her, as long as she cared for him, there could be no other lovers. She would have to accept and live with her blighted hopes.

'I'll have a shower,' he said casually, loosening his tie.

'Of course. The bathroom adjoining my bedroom ... our bedroom doesn't have a shower fixture, but the other bathroom does. I'll show you where it is.'

She led the way to the visitors' room, decorated in spring-green and white.

Glancing at the two single beds with their white cane headboards and tailored green linen covers, he asked, 'Are there twin beds in our room?'

'No, a double.'

She wondered if he took it for granted that he was not the first man to stay at the flat overnight. He had never asked about her past. Perhaps he didn't care what she had done, or not done, before he'd entered her life.

The towels for her visitors' use were stacked on white open shelves alongside the hand-basin counter. She took down a large green bath sheet and a small towel and hung them on the rail within reach of the shower compartment.

'I'll leave you to choose your soap. There are some unscented tablets,' she said, indicating a wicker basket containing an assortment of soaps from several countries.

'How about joining me?' he suggested, standing in the doorway in his shirt-sleeves—he must have discarded his coat as they'd come through the bedroom—and beginning to unbutton his cuffs.

'I—er—don't want to get my hair wet,' she answered, beginning to blush. 'I only use the shower when I shampoo. Otherwise I have baths. I'm afraid it isn't the kind of bath which people can share,' she added, striving to sound more self-possessed than she felt.

'Mm...pity.' He remained on the threshold, blocking her exit, smiling slightly. 'If I'm through before you are, is there room for me to come and talk to you?'

She wasn't sure if he was serious or taking a gentle rise out of her.

'Of course.'

Still he didn't move out of the way. He was undoing his front buttons now, revealing a muscular chest still brown from its last exposure to the sun.

'Are you shy of me, Flower?' he asked softly.

'I...yes, I suppose I am...a little.'

He pulled his shirt free of his trousers. 'Let's do something to break the ice, then.'

His next movement was to reach for her.

Swept into his powerful embrace for the first time since his return from America, she instinctively closed her eyes against the sight of his tall head swooping towards her. Then his lips were warm on her mouth and her mind became empty of thought as he gave her a long sensuous kiss.

'Is that better?' he asked presently, nuzzling the side of her neck, his hands sliding over her back, pressing her to him more closely.

Her reply was a dazed wordless murmur.

He took hold of her wrists and put her arms round his neck. Then he kissed her again, for a long time, until she forgot everything but the physical pleasure of being firmly held by strong arms while his lips moved slowly on hers.

When he raised his head and put her away from him, she was reluctant to come down to earth.

'Go and have your bath now,' he told her, his voice husky.

Ten minutes later, after a quick immersion in warm scented water, Flower had brushed her teeth and now was brushing her hair at the counter in her bathroom when he joined her.

She was wearing her towelling robe, loosely sashed. He had a towel wrapped round his hips and thighs. The splendour of his visible torso, on which there was neither surplus flesh nor over-developed sinews, but only the elastic muscles and taut skin of a naturally strong and fit man, sent a tremor of pleasure through her.

He took the brush from her hand and replaced it on the counter, sliding his arm round her waist and making her lean against him.

'I've been looking forward to this moment for a long time,' he said quietly.

And then he untied the sash and opened her robe, his blue eyes glittering as he studied her naked body in the mirror, her breasts, her navel, the still-damp tangle of curls at the junction of her thighs.

'Your body is as beautiful as your face,' he murmured close to her ear as he pulled the robe off her shoulders and made enough space between them for it to slide down her arms and slip to the floor. At the same time he loosened the towel he was wearing before once more drawing her against him, her bare back against his bare chest, the curves of her small, soft behind in contact with his long hard thighs.

She felt his pulsating virility, the hot and impatient life-force aroused by her nudity. But if the primitive male in him wanted to take her here and now, it was the civilised man who was in control. His hands, as he ran them over her in a long slow exploration were gentle. His fingertips touched her as carefully as if her tender flesh could be as easily damaged as the fragile porcelain petals on a rare piece of Chelsea she had once seen him handle.

'Do you like that?' he asked her, repeating a subtle caress.

She could only nod and close her eyes, made oddly shy by having to watch him make love to her.

'Let's go to bed.' With easy strength he picked her up, using one broad brown shoulder to push wide the half-open door and carry her through to the bed she had already turned down.

By late the next day, local time, they had reached their destination, an island in the chain called the Grenadines.

There was nothing to do there but laze in the sun, swim, snorkel and stroll the vanilla sand beaches lapped by water shading from crystal to the dark blue of the deep ocean where local fishing boats, small freighters and yachtsmen sailed the channels between the reefs.

Flower had spent much of the flight dozing. For they hadn't slept much the night before. Roderick's ardour had seemed unquenchable. Over and over his desire for her had revived and he had made love yet again, every time exacting a wilder response from her. He hadn't reminded her in words of his promise to strip from her every last inhibition, but that was what he had done.

And now, as they looked round their bungalow, one of a small spread-out colony of bedrooms with bathrooms and verandas, she sensed that it wouldn't be long before he did it again.

'A swim first, I think, don't you?' he suggested.

She nodded and started to unpack.

Minutes later they were stepping out of their flip-flops at the water's edge before walking into a sea which instantly washed away the fatigue of the long flight from Europe and the wait at Barbados airport before the final short hop by small plane to the island.

The days that followed were punctuated by frequent dips in the sea, starting soon after sunrise when they had the beach to themselves, apart from a youth employed to rake up dead leaves from the machineel trees and sea grape bushes.

After bathing they would rinse off the salt water in the open-air shower enclosure at the back of their bungalow. Usually they showered together with the result that, although they had risen early, they invariably breakfasted late, and the sheets, changed every day, were afterwards so wildly rumpled that Flower would surreptitiously straighten them before the maid came to collect them.

Often, as they ate their breakfast and she felt the amazing glow of well-being which followed these interludes, she was tempted to lean towards him and put her hand on his brown wrist and blurt out the truth: 'Roderick . . . I love you!'

What restrained her was the belief that such an admission could only be an embarrassment to him.

* * *

As well as swimming with him before breakfast,
after watching him run back and forth along the
beach the first day, Flower started running herself.
Knowing she would not be able to keep up with
him at first, she set off in the opposite direction
and finished a couple of lengths in the time it took
him to run four.

Afterwards they would swim again to cool off—
for even at that early hour the exercise made their
skins glisten—and then sit at the water's edge, enjoying the changing colours of the cloudscape.

They had been on the island a week when, during
one of these early-morning sky-watches, she realised
that in a few hours their honeymoon would pass
the halfway point. Then, thinking regretfully of
having to return to winter weather and everyday
life, she was reminded of a remark made by Kim
on the day of her arrival which Flower had not
queried at the time but had not fully understood.

'What did Kim mean by saying it was she who
got you interested in the connection between junk
food and delinquent behaviour?' she asked.

Roderick's dark eyebrows contracted. 'When did
she tell you that?'

'The day she descended on us.'

His long brown legs with their light covering of
dark hair had been stretched out in front of him.
Now he drew them up, resting his crossed forearms
on his knees.

'It's been known for a long time that there's a
tie-up between certain foods and certain physical
conditions,' he said. 'People who suffer from
migraine learn to avoid chocolate and oranges.
Other people develop rashes after eating dairy
products. At the beginning of the Eighties, a New

Zealand nutritionist working in California became convinced that, in many cases, unruly and criminal behaviour is caused by a poor diet.'

Flower had been lying on her back, one arm under her head to protect her wet hair from getting sandy, although before they returned to their bungalow they would both rinse the sand from their bodies under the open-air shower where the garden met the beach.

As she sat up, Roderick went on, 'In certain people, refined sugar causes blood-sugar abnormalities which, in turn, are thought to cause hooliganism and crime. The average sugar intake in Western countries is a hundred pounds a year. Lots of young people without proper cooking facilities eat as much as a pound a day, most of it "hidden" in junk food, which also contains a lot of salt.'

His mention of junk food reminded her of the conversation at dinner the night they had met.

'But these are just theories, aren't they?' she asked.

'By no means. Studies in the States show that at least eighty per cent of young delinquents have hypoglycaemia which alters the function of the brain in a way linked to bad behaviour and substance-abuse... drugs, glue-sniffing and so on.'

He glanced at her and smiled. 'But I don't imagine that's of much interest to you.'

She said crisply, 'Don't patronise me, Roderick. I'm not stupid... or indifferent.'

'I wasn't suggesting you were. But I know I can be a bore when I get on my hobby-horse. I've seen people's eyes start to glaze,' he said drily. 'I've learned not to ride it except among those who share the obsession.'

'But I'm your wife. We're supposed to be sharing everything.'

'Up to a point. It doesn't mean you have to pay rapt attention to my every utterance. In public—yes. That's different. But in private—no. To bore an acquaintance is bad enough. To bore one's partner is more serious.'

'Is that an oblique hint that some of my conversation bores you?'

He laughed. 'It hasn't so far, but I may as well warn you now that if you ever try to induce me to go clothes-shopping with you I'll put up serious resistance. Maybe European women don't take their husbands along as often as North Americans.'

'Some of them do. But I shan't. For one thing you'll be too busy, and, anyway, I trust my own judgement. But that's getting away from what we were talking about. If you are seriously interested in the connection between junk food and delinquency, why aren't you doing something about it instead of founding a clinic to help stressed business tycoons?'

Roderick rolled on to his front, propping himself on his elbows and sifting the fine coral sand through his long fingers. It was a posture which reminded her of the way, in the aftermath of love, he would stroke her hair off her forehead and drop gentle kisses on her closed eyelids, closed because she dared not let him see the sadness she felt because he had never said, perhaps never would say, 'I love you.'

Now he was silent for so long that she thought he might be ignoring her question. Until, suddenly, he said, 'I have plans to do something about it. But one has to be practical. When the clinic for businessmen is established and making a profit, then I shall have the resources to start another clinic for teenage junk-food addicts. It's no use attempting to do that without the means to fund it, and clearly it's not going to please your grandfather, who is one of the major suppliers of junk food.'

'I see. Does Kim know about this plan?'

'Yes; it's been in my mind a long time. I discussed it with George and with her, but it was only when my father died and the house became mine that I had the ideal place, if not the means, to set up such a clinic.'

'When were you planning to tell me...if I hadn't asked?'

'I couldn't see any point in dumping a conflict of interests on you while the plan was only a pipe-dream. Our relationship has its own complications. Do we need to address problems which aren't even in blueprint yet?'

'I don't like being excluded from anything which is important to you. Would you like it if I had secrets?'

As she said it she thought, But you wouldn't want to know the only thing I am keeping from you.

'It isn't a secret, Flower...never has been.' He stopped playing with the sand and with one lithe movement sprang up. 'Let's go and eat.'

After breakfast one of the islanders took them and two other couples snorkelling. So far, no one had guessed that she and Roderick were honeymooners.

The boat trip included a picnic lunch in the shade of an awning rigged on a tiny islet by the boatman.

Listening in silence while her husband chatted to the others, Flower was glad that he had a more serious purpose in life than merely making money and preserving his heritage.

That evening, while they were strolling along the moonlit beach after dinner, she said, 'Would you really have thrown us out if I hadn't agreed to marry you?'

'To throw out suggests a heartless eviction of people with nowhere to go,' said Roderick. 'It wouldn't have been like that. Your grandfather is a multi-millionaire. He would have had no difficulty in finding somewhere else to live. The manor is only a status symbol to him. There are plenty of others around.'

'But it means more than that to me . . . I love the house. It's my home. I've probably spent more time there than you have.'

He put a hand on her shoulder and turned her to face him.

'Is that why you married me, Flower?'

He had his back to the moon and his face was in shadow. She could not read his expression or deduce from the tone of his voice whether the question was prompted by idle curiosity or whether her motive for marrying him was a matter of much deeper interest.

'No, it wasn't,' she answered. 'To marry a man for his house—however beautiful—would be crazy. I won't deny that I'm glad I'm going to go on living there, but that wasn't the reason I agreed to marry you.'

'What was?'

For a moment she was tempted to answer him honestly; to admit the depth of her feelings for him.

Instead, after a pause, she said lightly, 'Perhaps instinct told me that you would be a brilliant lover. As I don't believe in adultery, it was an important consideration.'

'In that case, I'm surprised you didn't check out my prowess beforehand,' he said drily.

'I've always trusted my instinct. It's never let me down yet.'

She stepped out of her sandals and bent to pick them up, intending to walk through the crystalline shallows, putting an end to a line of conversation she regretted having started.

As she straightened, the sandals dangling from her fingers by their heel-straps, Roderick moved closer.

'My instinct told me the same thing about you,' he said. 'The night you came down to the morning-room and ran away, you weren't running away from me but from your own feelings, weren't you?'

'Perhaps...I can't really remember.'

'Can't you?' He put his hands on her waist, caressing it with his palms. 'I think you can. I think you remember that night as clearly as I do, but you still can't bring yourself to admit that you wanted me as much as I wanted you. Why not, I wonder?'

It was easy to avoid answering this awkward question. She had only to lift her face and part her lips to make his light hold tighten possessively, his dark head swoop towards hers.

Although it was possible there might be people watching them, she abandoned herself to his kiss, not caring who saw them embracing. Nor did she protest when he swung her up in his arms and carried her across the beach and along the path to their bungalow.

In their bedroom, the curtains had already been drawn by the maid while they'd been dining. But they didn't shut out the moonlight, which filtered through the filmy material, turning the room into a silver cave. And there was something of the caveman in the way Roderick tossed her on to the centre of the bed—fortunately it had a well-sprung mattress on a padded base—and began to tear off his clothes.

Flower sat up and pulled her loose printed voile top over her head. It was airy but not too see-through and she wasn't wearing a bra. The matching culottes had a waistband of stretchy shirring. She pulled it down over her hips, taking her panties with it and swiftly discarding both garments.

Then she lay back, naked and motionless, waiting for Roderick to do whatever he wished with her.

Silhouetted against the bright backdrop of the translucent curtains, he looked very tall and powerful, wide shoulders tapering to lean hips and long, hard thighs.

Stooping, his hands grasped her knees and swept them apart. He plunged forward. But instead of the rapid possession she expected, the rough, even brutal coupling for which he was clearly ready, she found herself clasped in his arms and rolled over until it was he who was lying on his back with her softer, slighter body balanced on his.

'I want you . . . God, how I want you.' The words were a husky murmur from deep in his throat.

And then she was seated astride him, their bodies joined in a wild, rhythmic, sensual tango, her spine arched, her head flung back, her mind oblivious to everything but the subtle, irresistible mastery of his touch on all her most sensitive places.

Time and again he drove her to panting, shuddering ecstasy until she felt drained and exhausted. Only then, when she collapsed on his chest, her whole body throbbing and quivering, did he reverse their positions and with long slow thrusts and extraordinarily erotic kisses begin to set fire to her senses, making her nerve-ends sizzle and burn like slow fuses.

When the flashpoint came, it was the most wonderful sensation she had ever experienced, lasting longer than before and, as it slowly subsided, bringing the prickle of tears to her closed eyelids. Surely, she thought as their bodies relaxed, surely if they could share these intimate physical delights the time must come when their minds would be equally in harmony?

Late the following afternoon, she woke up from a nap—the result of spending the morning on waterskis followed, after lunch, by a repetition of last night's lovemaking—to find Roderick no longer beside her. He was outside, on the veranda, reading what looked like a letter.

When she went outside he said, 'This is a fax from Kim. She's still in England...wants to stay.'

He handed over the facsimile of a typed letter. But 'Dear Roderick' and 'Yours affectionately, Kim' had been written by hand.

Flower's heart sank as she read the typed part in which Kim said he would be glad to hear she had asked for and been granted an immediate release from her present post in order to help Roderick launch his clinic.

'Did she discuss this with you? Did you know what she was going to do?'

'No, she didn't, and I'm not sure that it's a wise move to uproot herself. But, of course, she'll be a great asset. She's extremely good at her job, or was before George's death threw her whole life out of kilter.'

Flower remembered what her grandfather had said about Kim. Perhaps it wasn't true. Perhaps it was. Either way, she didn't relish the prospect of having Kim around on a permanent basis.

But, afraid that Roderick would think her uncharitable, she kept her misgivings to herself.

Once they got back from their honeymoon, everything changed.

Matters relating to the clinic occupied almost all Roderick's time. Often, when they were together, he was exasperated by delays and unforeseen snags. Although he was good at handling people and would have made an excellent diplomat, his energy and efficiency were such that it was hard for him to bear patiently with muddles and mistakes caused by others' lack of those qualities.

He did not take it out on Flower when he was annoyed, but neither was she the confidante of his troubles. He talked them over with Kim, and Flower felt that the bond between them was growing daily stronger while her own relationship with him seemed at a standstill.

Only in bed, in his arms, was she able to nourish the illusion that they would one day be lovers in the fullest sense. For, even if their minds were not, their bodies were perfectly attuned.

But even that changed as the weeks passed. Once the final ecstasy was over and they were lying breathless and spent, their heartbeats beginning to slow down, he did not remain in her arms as he had on the island.

Now he moved away almost at once. They never went to sleep entwined. And often, instead of sleeping, she would lie awake, locked in a loneliness she had never felt before she was married.

Another worry was her grandfather's health. By now Stephen had proved that, left to his own devices, he could handle the responsibility, and it was changing his character. As his confidence in himself grew, his progress-reports to Abel became less full and less frequent.

'I want to know what's going on,' her grandfather fumed. 'If he doesn't come round tonight, tomorrow I'm going to the works.'

'You know what it would do to your blood-pressure, Dodo. Stephen can't come tonight. He's taking Sharon out to dinner,' Flower reminded him.

She thought it right that her brother should give most of his spare time to his wife and children and only come to the manor to bring the old man up to date once or twice a week. It was Abel who was being unreasonable, to the detriment of his damaged heart.

This anxiety came to a climax when the middle-aged secretary, who had been Abel's right hand, asked for indefinite leave to look after the elder brother with whom she lived and who was seriously ill.

Stephen, who had found her a trial, promptly offered her early retirement on a good pension. But engaging a personal assistant to replace her was harder than he had anticipated.

'Why not get Flower to help you until you can find someone suitable?' Roderick suggested when Stephen mentioned this difficulty.

'Me?' she exclaimed in surprise.

'Why not? You know more about the business than a new PA would at first. You have some computer skills. You could hold the fort quite effectively, I should have thought.'

'That's not a bad idea, Rod,' said her brother. 'Yeah...why not? Let's give it a go.'

So, for the first time in her life, Flower started going out to work, and found it an effective distraction from her personal problems.

What surprised her was how easy it was for someone with common sense and the skills required to supervise the running of a large house to pick up the not dissimilar techniques involved in being Stephen's assistant.

Because she thought it inappropriate to arrive at the works in her scarlet Ferrari, she arranged for her brother to pick her up in the morning, and she dressed in her most discreet clothes: pleated skirts, blazers and white or cream shirts. She even modified her hairstyle, brushing it close to her head and twisting it into a neat coil. She made a point of not wearing her engagement ring or any striking jewellery. Perhaps she was overdoing the understatement, but she felt it was the best way to get it across that she was a serious person, not the frivolous butterfly the other staff might perceive her to be.

Among her duties was the preliminary interviewing of the applicants for the post she was filling temporarily. Although the salary was good with lots of additional perks, there were not many of them. For some reason the job wasn't attracting the kind of girl Stephen wanted.

'Maybe you should think about staying on permanently,' he said to her after yet another applicant had failed to satisfy Flower that she could hold down the job. 'We make a good team, you and I.'

Flower smiled and agreed that they did, but didn't commit herself. She had already missed one period. She hadn't mentioned it to Roderick and he had too much on his mind to have thought about it himself. But, if she was pregnant already, she would keep it to herself until there was more conclusive evidence.

Often when she got home Roderick and Kim were still busy. In any case, her grandfather insisted that she go straight to him and describe the events of the day. Only when he had questioned her was she free to go to her room to bath and change for the evening.

At first Kim had made a point of discreetly absenting herself from their part of the house in the evening. But as time went on she spent more and more time in their company, perhaps at Roderick's invitation as the two of them never seemed to tire of talking shop.

Most of the time Flower put up with this without comment. But sometimes, at the end of a tiring day when she longed for a quiet evening alone with no one but Roderick there, it was hard to endure Kim's presence.

One evening, when Kim had finally taken herself off to bed, she was driven to say, 'I wonder if there's something Kim dislikes about her own sitting-room. She doesn't seem to make much use of it.'

She had tried not to sound sarcastic but evidently hadn't succeeded.

Roderick gave her one of his keen looks. 'She can't bear to be on her own. It's a phase most widows go through. Bear with her, Flower. She's had a tough break.'

'I know . . . and I'm very sorry for her.'

But I want to be alone with you sometimes, was her silent rider. Oh, Roderick, what's happening to us? We're growing further apart, not closer.

That night, for the first time, he did not make love to her. Not because he was tired. When she had finished in the bathroom she found him reading a thriller by a highly praised crime-writer.

Flower climbed into the high four-poster built to accommodate the long legs of one of his equally tall forebears. It was so high off the ground that, on her side, a step was necessary.

Her arrival did not disturb him, for the bed was as wide as it was long, requiring specially made sheets and an emperor-sized duvet.

There were always books on Flower's night-table and a stack of glossy magazines, although since her marriage she had done little reading in bed. She picked up a copy of *House Beautiful*, an American decorating monthly recommended by Kim and on sale in London.

But, although she had flipped through it quickly and knew it was full of good ideas and attractive colour schemes, none of the articles in it grabbed her attention. Not because they weren't interesting but because it was the first time she had come to bed and not found Roderick waiting to make love.

She had realised that it had had to come, this night when he preferred to read rather than to caress her. But surely, if he had been beginning to care for her, he would have glanced up from his thriller and smiled at her? Or reached for her hand and held it till he needed to turn a page? Or shifted sideways until their arms were touching?

Presently Roderick yawned, put a marker in his book and turned out the light on his side of the canopied bed.

'Goodnight.' He lay down on his side, facing away from her.

'Goodnight.'

She forced herself to read an article about the beautiful simple furniture and household goods made by the Shakers from the beginning of the nineteenth century until the American Civil War. But it was an effort to concentrate and she knew by tomorrow she would have forgotten most of it.

Her mind was too full of misery to grapple with anything but the fear that her marriage was already falling apart and it was not her but Kim who should be sharing Roderick's bed.

The date when her next period was due went by without anything happening. Her bra began to feel slightly tight, and one night, when Roderick came into the bathroom while she was brushing her teeth and would have unwrapped the towel she was wearing sarong-fashion, he suddenly changed his mind and confined himself to a friendly pat on her bottom.

She would not have rebuffed him, but he must have sensed that she wasn't in the mood, partly because her breasts felt swollen and tender. There was now no doubt in her mind that she was pregnant, but she felt that the news would keep.

The next symptom of her condition was a tendency to feel queasy. One morning, soon after she arrived at the works, she had to dash to her brother's private wash-room.

Stephen saw her emerge. He said, 'I recognise that pale-green look. Sharon had it when Matt was on the way. You're preggers, aren't you?'

Flower nodded. 'But don't tell Sharon yet. I haven't told Roderick.'

She felt all right for the rest of the morning, but after lunch felt queasy again. There was no urgent work to be dealt with. In spite of her protests, Stephen insisted on running her home.

'Tell Rod, then I can tell Shar. And ring up your medic to get it officially confirmed.'

His protective attitude touched her. She wondered how Roderick would react.

She found him in the office he shared with Kim. Later, when the alterations and new buildings were complete, they would have separate offices.

Instead of being at their desks, working, they were at the far end of the room by the window-seat, but not sitting on it, taking a coffee break. They were on their feet, locked in a close embrace, fused into a single silhouette against the bright light outside.

The American had her head pressed against Roderick's shoulder, and his head was bowed over hers. Every line of their bodies expressed an intimate tenderness. No one, seeing them like this, caught unawares, could have doubted that they were lovers.

Flower wanted to turn away, to run, to escape the painful proof of what, deep down, she had feared since Kim's arrival.

But she found herself unable to move, powerless to avert her eyes from the sight of the man she loved holding the woman he really wanted.

As she stared at them, all her hopes and dreams for the future crumbling into dust, Roderick lifted his head and turned his face towards her.

'Flower... you're back early.'

CHAPTER TEN

RODERICK sounded surprised to see Flower, but not noticeably embarrassed.

It was Kim who was startled, whose head came away from his shoulder with a nervous jerk and who broke their embrace with a hasty step backwards.

Considering the turmoil inside her, Flower was amazed to hear herself say in a calm voice, 'Perhaps it's just as well.'

She closed the door behind her and walked towards them. A few moments ago her instinct had been to run, to put off the moment of truth. But already she knew there was no escape from this situation. It had to be confronted...now.

As she approached, Kim turned away and made some furtive movements, which Flower took to be an attempt to wipe off badly smudged lipstick.

But, if a few minutes earlier they had been exchanging passionate kisses, there were no traces of colour on or around Roderick's lips. And he seemed as composed as if she had found them engaged in some mundane discussion to do with the clinic.

'You look pale, Flower. Are you all right?' he asked as she stopped about six feet away from him.

The question amazed her. How could she be all right with her marriage in ruins? Did he think that she wouldn't care if they split up?

Before she could reply, Kim turned round. It was immediately obvious that she had been crying; not merely shedding a few tears, but weeping with an abandonment which had swollen her eyelids, reddened her nose and streaked her cheeks.

Roderick said, 'Kim is going back to the US. Coming here hasn't helped. She's been trying to convince herself that it was a good idea, but this morning a letter from her mother made her unbearably homesick.'

Her eyes awash with fresh tears, Kim said in a quavery voice, 'I don't want to let Roderick down, but I have to go home. I should never have come in the first place. I'm sorry, Flower.'

Flower said nothing. Was it possible that she had completely misinterpreted the scene which had met her eyes when she'd opened the door?

It seemed that it was, for now Roderick was replacing his arm around Kim's shoulders and, as she began to weep again, sending his wife a silent but unmistakable signal.

Plainly it meant: I need help here!

Her thoughts still in great confusion, she obeyed the deep-seated instinct to comfort someone in distress—even a woman towards whom, a few moments ago, she had felt strong hostility.

'Come and sit down, Kim. Roderick, could you organise some tea, please? I could do with a cup myself,' she said, steering the American to the nearby window-seat.

'Are you certain this bout of homesickness isn't just a passing mood, Kim?' she went on as he left the room.

The other girl made a strong effort to pull herself together. 'It was a mistake to come. I see that now. I was running away...and you can't run away from your deepest feelings. There's no escape...no quick cure. I should have known that. Missing my family only makes it worse. You and Roderick have been wonderful to me, but I should never have inflicted myself on you. It was selfish to burden you with my unhappiness.'

It would have been hypocritical for Flower to deny that Kim's presence had not been a burden. To her, if not to Roderick, it had been a constant shadow over her peace of mind.

She said, 'You've been a great help to Roderick, in these early stages of getting the clinic organised, but they do say that it's a mistake for people who've been bereaved to make any major changes in the way they live for at least a year or two. I did wonder if it was wise for you to uproot yourself, even to come and work with a close friend.'

'It was crazy,' Kim admitted. 'My parents tried to dissuade me, but I wouldn't listen.'

'I'll be honest with you,' said Flower. 'I thought, when you first arrived here and seemed upset that our marriage had been put forward, that you might have been hoping that Roderick would...would fill the void in your life.'

Kim flushed. 'I—I did hope that for a while...before I came to England. I knew Roderick would never love me in the way George did, but I thought our work and our friendship would be enough to make it a workable partnership. And then somehow I had the idea that you weren't in love with him...that you only wanted to be Lady Anstruther. But I didn't realise my antipathy showed that clearly.'

'Pretty clearly,' Flower said drily.

'I'm sorry, Flower. I was wrong about you. After you came back from your wedding trip I began to see I had been mistaken. But you British keep your deepest emotions so buttoned-up. It took me a while to grasp that Roderick was crazy about you and you felt the same about him.'

After a pause, Flower said carefully, 'How did we give ourselves away?'

'One day I said something about you...about your not having a career...which Roderick interpreted as a criticism. It was the first time he'd ever been angry with me. Later, when I'd explained that I hadn't meant to sound critical, he told me about falling in love with you almost from the moment he met you. He said he knew right away...well, within a couple of hours...that you were the girl he'd been looking for.'

'He did?' Flower hoped she didn't sound as astonished as she felt.

'And then, as I got to know you better,' Kim went on, 'I began to see through your reserve, to recognise the signs that, although you were never demonstrative the way Americans are when they love someone, you weren't really cold and stand-offish. That was just a façade.'

'It certainly was! I love Roderick with all my heart. It was love at first sight for me too,' Flower admitted.

'I'm glad,' said Kim. 'I really am. George and I always hoped that Roderick would find the kind of happiness we had...if only briefly,' she added with a deep sigh.

'You'll find happiness again...one day,' Flower said gently. 'It may not be the same way you were happy before, but surely love is like...' she paused, searching for an appropriate simile '...like music or art or any of life's richest experiences? The important thing is to have the capacity to care for another person. I don't think everyone does and that's why marriages go wrong, because one or both partners *can't* love, in the same way that some people lack an ear for music or an eye for beauty. But, if you know that you *can* love another person, then sooner or later there will be someone else for you.'

Kim nodded. 'I guess so. But it's hard to adjust to being alone when you've known what it is to be half of a pair. I'll feel better when I've washed my face. I'll be right back.'

When she had gone, Flower remained on the window-seat, coming to terms with the fact that Roderick had told Kim that he had fallen in love within hours of returning to the manor. Now what she longed to know was why he had never admitted it.

A few minutes later he returned. 'Where's Kim?'

'Washing her face.'

He scrutinised Flower's face before saying, 'You look better than you did when you arrived. You looked like a ghost when you came in.'

'I didn't feel well this morning. In fact, I threw up my breakfast. I think I'm probably pregnant.'

He nodded. 'That thought had crossed my mind. How do you feel about it?'

She said, 'I'm not keen on the morning sickness, if that's what it is, but apart from that I'm delighted. How else would I feel?'

'You might not like the idea of gradually losing your figure…of being, as it were, taken over. When it comes to the point, women have all kinds of reactions.'

'Well, yes... depending on their circumstances. But if they're the loving wife of a loving husband, with no housing or financial problems, I should think most of them feel pleased. Or am I deluding myself that, even if you never actually say so, you have become rather fond of me?'

His eyes flashed with a light which was new to her. He reached out as if to take her by the shoulders. But at that point there was a discreet cough, and they turned to see John coming in with a tray of tea things.

Before he had set them out to his satisfaction, Kim returned.

As she poured out tea, drank it and slowly ate a plain biscuit, Flower was aware of Roderick's suppressed impatience to continue the conversation the footman had interrupted.

Instead of which he was obliged to discuss Kim's return to her homeland.

'The sooner the better, I think, now that I've come to my senses... unless you would like me to stay until you've found a replacement. But I shouldn't think that will take long. There must be any number of British nutritionists who would jump at the chance to assist you,' she said.

'No, I don't think that will be a problem.'

Kim didn't seem to notice that his answer sounded *distrait*, but Flower did. Her cup of tea drunk, she said, 'I'll leave you two to get on while I go and have a chat with Dodo, if he isn't napping. See you later.'

But before she was halfway along the corridor she heard the door open behind her and was commanded to wait.

She checked and half turned. 'Yes?'

He came striding towards her. 'I want to talk to you...privately...in our room.'

She had an impulse to tease him. 'Can't it wait till later?'

'No, it can't.' He placed the flat of his hand against the small of her back and propelled her forward.

As they walked briskly through the house, heading for their bedroom, she began to feel more and more excited about what he would say and do when they got there.

The first thing he did was to turn the key in the lock, as if they had come upstairs to make love, although going to bed in the daytime had stopped when they'd come back from their honeymoon.

When she would have moved away to her dressing-table, he caught her by the wrist and swung her to face him.

'A little while ago you accused me of never expressing my feelings for you,' he said curtly.

'It wasn't an accusation, Roderick. Merely a statement of fact. Why has it made you angry?'

'Because...because lately, dammit, you've been so offhand that I felt the last thing you wanted was any soul-baring from me.'

'Offhand? How unfair! And untrue! I would have made love every night if you'd wanted me. I have never, ever made an excuse...pleaded a headache...said I was too tired.'

'Oh, you like sex. I can't fault you there. But I happen to want rather more than your beautiful body. You see, I'm not what you called "rather fond" of you. I'm head over heels in love with you, and have been from the beginning.'

The last shred of doubt in her mind was swept away by this unequivocal statement.

'Then why on earth didn't you say so?' she exclaimed. 'It is still a male prerogative to make the first move, you know.'

'But not without some encouragement.'

'If you'll unshackle my wrist I'll give you some encouragement.'

Perhaps unaware of the painful strength of his grip, at once he released it.

Flower moved closer and put her arms round his neck. 'I love you, Roderick. If I've seemed offhand it's because I've been deeply unhappy...longing for you to feel the way about me that I feel about you. Until this afternoon, when Kim told me, I had no idea that what happened to me when you came here had also happened to you. How could I know that? I believed that, on your side, ours was a marriage of convenience.'

'Not true! It's been driving me crazy...thinking that was *your* motive...that the only thing about me you were in love with was my house.'

'Well, I am...I admit it. I adore this house...but I love its owner far more. If we had to live somewhere else...start from scratch in a semi-detached, that would be just fine with me. Oh, Roderick, please say it again...that you love me...you really do love me.'

He took her face between his hands. 'I love you...and always will. It's a family trait. Almost all the Anstruther men have been faithful, devoted husbands.'

'I can't say the same for my family. Their history isn't recorded as far back as yours, but all the ones I do know about have had terrible cat-and-dog

marriages. But I'm going to change that pattern,'
she told him, her eyes bright with happiness.

Later, before they went down to join the others,
Flower opened the drawer in her dressing-table
where she kept the pendant Roderick had given her
on their wedding-day.

'Put it on for me, will you, darling?' she said,
holding it out to him.

'I thought, as you never wore it, you didn't like
it,' he said as he fastened the chain.

'It's beautiful, but I found I couldn't bear to wear
it when what it symbolised seemed forever out of
reach.'

'I've forgotten what you said the tree was
called . . . and you never did tell me the story behind
it.'

'It's called the singing tree, and the legend is that
it grows on a mysterious island which everyone
would like to find because anyone who does also
finds all their heart's desires. Obviously the story
is an allegory; the singing tree is love.'

A year later Kim came to spend a few days with
them en route to a medical conference in Paris. This
time Flower was able to welcome her without con-
straint, secure in the confidence that she was deeply,
passionately loved.

As she showed off her baby daughter, who had
inherited her blonde hair and Roderick's blue eyes,
she wondered if it caused Kim pain to see her so
happy when she was still on her own. But at least
her job brought her into contact with lots of men
and perhaps she would meet someone at the
conference.

'I thought Roderick might be disappointed at not having a son and heir, but he adores Lily,' she told Kim. 'And we hope to have another next year.'

Later, when Roderick returned from attending a meeting in London sponsored by the World Health Organisation, she was glad when he greeted Kim warmly. It seemed very strange that she could ever have been jealous of the American.

All the confusions and doubts of the early days of her marriage seemed a long time ago.

'And how are you, dearest girl?' he asked, as he did every evening when his day's work was over and they were both at leisure to enjoy each other's company.

He had been away overnight and she knew by the glint in his eyes that, in spite of the presence of a guest, he wouldn't be sitting up late, discussing the progress of the clinic or the latest attempts by the spokesmen for the sugar industry to dismiss the results of research by the anti-sugar lobbies.

Once dinner was over, and the main news telecast, he would smother a yawn, claim tiredness and sweep her upstairs, there to demonstrate that in fact his reserves of energy were far from exhausted.

'I'm fine,' she said, smiling up at him, silently answering the signal he was sending. 'Dodo is fine. Lily's fine. But we've missed you.'

'I missed you too.'

She knew he meant it.

As he turned away to concentrate on Kim, Flower lifted her hand to touch the piece of gold-ornamented malachite which now she wore nearly all the time, tucked inside cotton shirts by day, showing outside sweaters or silk tops by night. It had become her talisman, even more treasured than the Anstruther emerald which, one day, she hoped to pass on to the girl chosen by her son.

Many years ahead, the singing tree would go to Lily or perhaps to Lily's daughter. But that was far in the future, and meanwhile she hoped to have decades and decades of this marvellous, undeserved happiness with Lily's gorgeous father.

Where do you find hot Texas nights, smooth Texas charm and dangerously sexy cowboys?

COWBOYS AND CABERNET

Raise a glass—Texas style!

Tyler McKinney is out to prove a Texas ranch is the perfect place for a vineyard. Vintner Ruth Holden thinks Tyler is too stubborn, too impatient, too... Texas. And far too difficult to resist!

CRYSTAL CREEK reverberates with the exciting rhythm of Texas. Each story features the rugged individuals who live and love in the Lone Star State. And each one ends with the same invitation...

Y'ALL COME BACK... REAL SOON!

Don't miss *COWBOYS AND CABERNET* by Margot Dalton. Available in April wherever Harlequin books are sold.

Following the success of WITH THIS RING and
TO HAVE AND TO HOLD, Harlequin brings you

JUST MARRIED

SANDRA CANFIELD
MURIEL JENSEN
ELISE TITLE
REBECCA WINTERS

just in time for the 1993 wedding season!

Written by four of Harlequin's most popular authors, this
four-story collection celebrates the joy, excitement and
adjustment that comes with being "just married."

You won't want to miss this spring tradition, whether
you're just married or not!

AVAILABLE IN APRIL WHEREVER HARLEQUIN
BOOKS ARE SOLD

JM93

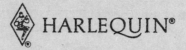

HARLEQUIN®

THE TAGGARTS OF TEXAS!

Harlequin's Ruth Jean Dale brings you
THE TAGGARTS OF TEXAS!

Those Taggart men—strong, sexy and hard to resist...

You've met Jesse James Taggart in FIREWORKS!
Harlequin Romance #3205 (July 1992)

And Trey Smith—he's THE RED-BLOODED YANKEE!
Harlequin Temptation #413 (October 1992)

And the unforgettable Daniel Boone Taggart in SHOWDOWN!
Harlequin Romance #3242 (January 1993)

Now meet Boone Smith and the Taggarts who started it all—
in LEGEND!
Harlequin Historical #168 (April 1993)

Read all the Taggart romances!
Meet all the Taggart men!

Available wherever Harlequin Books are sold.
